HOME RUN STRETCH

S. S. Gorman

PUBLISHED BY POCKET BOOKS

New York   London   Toronto   Sydney   Tokyo   Singapore

A MINSTREL PAPERBACK *ORIGINAL*

 A Minstrel Book published by
POCKET BOOKS, a division of Simon & Schuster
1230 Avenue of the Americas, New York, NY 10020

ISBN: 0-671-70382-X

First Minstrel Books printing March 1991

10 9 8 7 6 5 4 3 2 1

A MINSTREL BOOK and colophon are registered trademarks of Simon & Schuster.

Cover art by Bob Tanenbaum

Printed in the U.S.A.

HOME RUN
STRETCH

Chapter 1

THE LINEUP

Stretch Evans's brown eyes glistened with mischief. "Hey, guys, did you hear about the angel who lost his job?"

"Here we go again." Jack Klipp acted as if he weren't interested.

Chris Morton, Stretch's best friend in Conrad, Colorado, since the second grade, shrugged his shoulders. "Okay, I'll bite." The three sixth-graders were heading for their history class at Bressler Elementary. "What happened to the angel who lost his job?"

"He had *harp* failure," said Stretch.

Chris groaned. "That's terrible."

"It's worse than terrible. It's incredibly stupid," Jack added.

"No, it's not," the tall black boy said, laughing. "It's funny. Come on, you guys, where's your sense of humor?"

Jack ran his hand through his short, curly dark

brown hair. "I must've left it in science class with my funny bone."

Chris snickered.

"Oh, sure, laugh at *his* dumb joke," Stretch said. "Okay, how about this? If two's company and three's a crowd, what are four and five?"

"I don't know, what?" Chris said.

"Nine." Stretch slapped one of the metal lockers. "Pretty funny, huh?"

Jack stared at him. "You've totally lost it. You used to be kind of funny, but now you're a goner."

Chris elbowed the small, feisty twelve-year-old. "Ah, don't listen to Stretch. He's just hyper today because it's the first day of baseball practice."

"Yep, from now until the World Series in October I'll be making homers and signing autographs."

"Baseball is pretty cool," Jack agreed.

"Pretty cool? It's the coolest! Why do you think they call it the majors? It's majorly cool." Stretch swung at an imaginary ball and watched it sail high down the halls. "I can't wait for my tryout with the Cubs. On the other hand, maybe they'll just scout me in high school, and I can sign a million-dollar contract on the spot."

Jack leaned against the brick wall. "Pretty sure of yourself, aren't you?"

"He's good enough," Chris whispered. "He was the only fourth-grader two years ago to make the summer varsity league. All the rest of the guys were in junior high."

"Okay, I'm impressed, you're good. What position are you going to play this year?"

"Jump, dive, catch." Stretch leapt straight into the air to catch a pop fly only he could see. "Same as every year—left field."

"How about you, Morton?" Jack asked. "What position do you usually play?" Jack had only been friends with the guys since September.

"Oh, I bounce around a lot, but usually third or first."

"Yeah, I played third one summer," said Jack.

Stretch jumped in between the pair and threw an arm around each of them. "Then this year you can play third on our Bressler Elementary intramural team. My team."

"Man, we just finished basketball season at the Y two weeks ago."

Chris's sky-blue eyes gleamed. "With a pretty good record, too."

"Yeah, eight wins and three losses," Jack added, high-fiving first Chris, then Stretch.

Stretch nudged Jack. "So you finally admit you had fun playing basketball? Well, if you liked basketball, wait till you try baseball. It's even better."

Jack shifted his books to his other hip. "Yeah, I had fun, and you guys needed me. If I hadn't bailed you out, you would have lost even more games."

"I think you're forgetting I was top scorer," Stretch bragged, running ahead and shooting an imaginary basket.

3

Chris shook his head. "No, you weren't. Alex was."

"Alex doesn't count. She's a girl. She's not really one of the High-Fives."

"Don't tell her that." Chris bent over to take a long drink from the water fountain.

Jack defended Stretch. "He's talking about the club. She's not in the High-Fives club."

"At least *she* signed up for my baseball team. We need five more guys at least. Nine all together." Stretch ran his knuckles across the metal locker doors as they walked along.

"Gadget and J.R. are playing." Chris wiped his chin with the sleeve of his green sweater.

"J.R. will sign up for anything," Jack added.

Chris was quick to defend J.R., who was a year younger than the other High-Fives. "Oh, don't start that again. Just because J.R.'s your younger brother, you don't have the right to tell him what to do."

"Why not? It's been working great so far."

Stretch nudged his way between his friends again and slung his long arms over the shoulders of his shorter pals. "So, what's your excuse, Morton?"

"My folks are worried about my grades," Chris mumbled. "They say I've been spending more time playing games and hanging out than hitting the books."

"I thought your grades were okay," Stretch said.

"They are. Mostly B's and a few C's, but my mom says she'd like to see some A's."

Jack, who kept his good grades a secret, hoped to drop the discussion. "So, get 'em."

"Oh, sure, right." Chris sighed. "I'm not Gadget. I can't correctly quote every statistic known to man, and American history is going to be hard. We have Mr. Lehman, so we have to write a paper, you know."

Stretch snap-popped his fingers. "So write about the history of baseball. Lehman's the history teacher and the baseball coach. You'd have it made."

"Maybe that would work."

"On second thought, maybe it wouldn't," Stretch said.

"Why not? You just suggested it," Chris replied.

Stretch smiled. "Because I'm going to do it instead." He blocked the entrance to the classroom. "So, you guys in? I want to know before we go and see Coach Lehman. Come on, please."

Jack and Chris looked at each other. "Sure, if my folks don't make me quit," Chris said.

Jack nodded. "Yeah, anything you say. I found out during basketball, it's harder to fight you guys than to join you."

"Yes." Stretch jumped up and punched the air with his fist. "You won't regret it. I promise. That makes six. We can figure out the rest of the team at Mike's after practice today."

The guys walked into their classroom. Some of the kids were sitting on their desks. Others were running around. "What's up, Gadget?" Chris asked the pudgy kid with wire-rimmed glasses who was quietly sitting and reading in the front row. Gadget didn't look up but pointed to the blackboard, which said, "Mr. Lehman will not be here today. Miss Hyland will be substituting."

"So where is she?"

"Maybe Ron Porter and his gang scared her away," Jack said, referring to the sixth-grade bully and his friends who had history just before them. He slid into his assigned seat.

"If anybody could do it, those creeps could."

Stretch puffed up his chest and tried to imitate the tough sixth-grader. "Yeah, if you look up *bully* in the dictionary, it's got Ron Porter's picture next to the definition." As the bell rang and everyone kept talking, the door flung open and a petite woman burst into the room. Chris scrambled for his assigned seat, but Stretch slid into it first. He motioned for Chris to take his seat.

"What are you doing?" Chris whispered.

"Play along. This is going to be fun."

"Good afternoon, class. If you've read the board, you know that my name is Miss Hyland. Mr. Lehman had an emergency appendectomy this morning and will be out for a few weeks."

"Poor coach," Stretch whispered.

"He's doing fine, but I'll be taking over his classes until he returns." Stretch measured her up as she leaned back against the large wooden desk. She had short, curly black hair and dark eyes. He decided she had a big voice for such a shrimp. "It will take me a few days to get to know all of your names, so

6

please help me out and be patient while I'm taking roll."

"This is going to be great," Stretch whispered to Chris as he tapped his eraser on the top of the desk.

Miss Hyland held up the plastic-covered seating chart and walked up and down each aisle with long, brisk steps, calling each name. Finally she came to the front of Stretch's row. "William Shaw."

"Present," Gadget answered formally. "But you can call me Gadget."

"All right, Gadget. My, that's an unusual nickname."

"Gadget's an unusual guy," Stretch said loud enough for everyone to hear. They giggled.

Miss Hyland studied Stretch, four seats down, and then glanced at her seating chart. "Is that so, Mr. Morton?" The class tittered even louder, but Stretch kept a straight face. "We call him Gadget because he knows how all sorts of gadgets work, like computers and stuff. My nickname's Chris. It's short for Christopher." Again the kids laughed.

"Yes, I know." Miss Hyland sounded confused. She called the three people between Gadget and Stretch. "Cathy Sullivan . . . Tom English . . . Jenny Garvey." They all answered, "Here." Then she said, "And of course we all remember Chris Morton." The class really roared this time and startled Miss Hyland. She stared at Stretch, who was focusing on the blackboard with his hands folded on top of Chris's desk. If she had any idea about the prank, she didn't let on. The class calmed down and she continued reading off names. "Lauren Gibbs . . . Jack Klipp . . . Carrie Dilley . . . Stuart Evans . . ."

"Everybody calls him Stretch," Stretch said, interrupting. Chris lowered his head and rubbed at the scratches on the desktop. "You'd think they'd call him that only if he were tall, but his height's not the reason." The rest of the class didn't even try to hide their laughter now. "They call him Stretch because he's always tired, stretching and yawning, stuff like that."

"I see." Miss Hyland nodded. "Is that right, Stretch?"

Chris scratched his wavy blond hair. "I guess."

During the rest of roll call, the class giggled and joked around. They finally settled down when Miss Hyland started the lesson. She stuck to Mr. Lehman's lesson plan: Ben Franklin and the Revolutionary War. "Can anyone tell me what Ben Franklin did after he invented electricity?" The class was silent for a moment before Stretch shot up his hand. "Yes, Chris?"

"Nothing. He didn't do anything. He was too shocked." That was all it took; the class was howling now.

"Quiet down. Quiet down, please!" Miss Hyland shouted. The kids kept laughing until she pulled a whistle out of the top desk drawer and blasted it three times. "That's enough. I know it's fun to play tricks on a substitute teacher, but this has gone on long enough. Take out a piece of paper and a pencil. We're going to have a pop quiz." The class groaned.

"And the *real* Chris Morton better hope that the impostor sitting in his chair knows a lot about the *real* Ben Franklin, because this grade is going to count." Chris and Stretch exchanged glances. "I want to talk to both of you after class." Stretch groaned. This wasn't turning out to be funny after all.

Chapter 2

DOUBLE PLAY

"What happened?" Gadget asked Stretch and Chris as they shuffled out of history.

"Detention," Stretch grumbled.

"Bummer!" Jack cried. "I knew when she asked you to stay after class it wasn't going to be pretty."

"And on the first day of baseball practice, too." J. R. Klipp, who, except for his straight hair, looked like Jack's twin brother, joined the older boys by the door.

Stretch made a fist and slammed it into his palm. "I have to miss our first baseball practice. Man, this lady is really messing things up for me."

"I guess she felt messed up, too." Gadget pushed his wire-framed glasses up on his nose.

"Thanks a lot, Gadget," Stretch sneered.

J.R.'s dark brown eyes met Chris's. "What about you? Did you get detention, too?"

"Nah. Stretch told her I didn't have anything to do with it."

Stretch leaned against the wall. "I wish Coach Lehman was back. How long does it take to get over appendicitis?"

"It's not an illness," Gadget explained. "The appendix is an organ. If it gets inflamed or bursts, it has to be surgically removed. Recovery time varies, but I wouldn't expect to see him for at least a month."

"A month! What about baseball? I can't wait a month to play."

Chris tried to calm his friend. "I'm sure they have a substitute coach, Stretch."

"Well, I hope it's better than his history sub. She's a loser." The bell rang and the boys ran in separate directions for their classes.

Stretch sat in the cafeteria for detention and watched "his team" gather by the exit door before going to their first practice. Bressler Elementary had two official playing fields and four smaller practice fields. The High-Fives were going to be working out on one of the playing fields. It had a tall chain-link fence blocking off some bleachers and two areas that the teams called their dugouts. They were actually just benches between two fences. The outfield was outlined by a large hedge. Stretch had hit several balls over it the year before. As he fumbled with his pencil, he promised himself he'd hit even more with the High-Fives. Right then he just wished he were with them. He could see J.R. bouncing around like a pinball, his big mitt falling off his small hand. Chris was talking to Alex Tye, a tall girl with green eyes and a long blond braid falling down her thin back. She was a good athlete, and Stretch had told Chris she might even have a shot at pitcher. Gadget's sandy hair was sticking out of his Bressler Elementary baseball cap. And Jack was being Jack, first yelling at his younger brother and then walking behind the rest of the gang. Stretch wished he were with them. Why did he have to be indoors writing his spelling list twenty times? Actually, he knew the answer to that but didn't want to think about it. If he wrote really fast, he decided he could get it done in a half hour, and then he'd only miss half of practice. He hated Miss Hyland. Mr. Lehman was such a good teacher and an even better coach.

"What you in for?" A soft voice whispered from behind Stretch.

"Oh, hi, Leena," he said. Leena Tucker was a short, bouncy black girl in his English class. She had the longest eyelashes Stretch had ever seen. "I got caught playing a prank on Lehman's sub. What about you?"

"Chewing gum in music class."

"Man, they're getting tough."

"It's a rule, but I hated to throw out a new piece."

"Yeah, I know how that goes," Stretch agreed.

She looked around the large cafeteria. "Not many people today."

Stretch leaned his chin on his hand. "It's the first day of spring ball."

"Oh, you're so good you won't miss anything."

Stretch perked up. "You've seen me play?"

12

"Lots of times."

Stretch didn't think much of girls. He thought they giggled too much and hung around when you were trying to be with the guys, but maybe Leena was different. At least she knew he was good at baseball. "Hey, Leena, who called for his pipe, his bowl, and a six-pack of soda pop?"

Leena wrinkled her nose. "I don't know, who?"

"Old King Cola."

Leena forgot where she was and laughed out loud.

"This is detention, not a social club," Miss Dean snapped.

Stretch pulled out some paper while Leena took a seat at the next table. "Talk to you later." She winked at him.

Stretch hurried to work on the assignment. He had a hard time concentrating, especially with the sound of baseballs cracking against hard wooden bats. He could almost smell the leather gloves and feel the grass grind into the knees of his faded jeans as he slid into home. His fingers cramped around the pencil as he tried to finish the next line. The more he hurried, the less he got done. The minutes ticked by rapidly, and the first half hour rushed by. His handwriting got worse. He hoped Miss Dean wouldn't make him do it over again.

"Here, Miss Dean. I finished. May I be excused, please?"

The teacher looked at the papers and frowned. "Well, you wouldn't get an A for penmanship, but

13

since this is your first offense this spring, you may be excused.''

Stretch didn't wait for another word but spun around and ran to the exit. He pulled his baseball cap and glove out of his pack and darted for the practice field.

"Stretch, over here." J.R.'s straight, dark brown hair floated in the spring breeze.

Chris slapped him on the back. "You must have broken a speed-writing record to get here this fast."

"Let's play ball!" Stretch screamed. "Where's the rest of the team?"

"With our coach working on ground balls."

"So introduce me to our fearless leader. He must've wondered where his star player was. Did you explain why I was going to be late?"

Gadget looked at Chris and Jack. "We didn't think that would be necessary."

"It's Mr. Quinn from social studies, right?"

Jack scuffed his toe into the grass. "Not exactly."

"Prrt, prrt, prrt." The whistle blasted three times, and the boys spun around to face their new coach.

Stretch's mouth dropped open wide. "Miss Hyland?"

"Welcome to spring ball, Mr. Evans. It is Mr. Evans now, right?"

"Right." Stretch felt his face get warm.

"We're about to work on defense; why don't you join the rest of the team." Stretch was still stunned but nodded.

"We were just as shocked as you are," Chris whispered.

"She can't be the coach. She's a girl. We want to win, not be the laughingstock of the whole school."

Jack agreed. "That's what I said. Ron Porter and his Raiders are going to have a field day with this."

"Well, she's not going to be my coach. She'll ruin my game. I'll complain to management. I'm going to ignore her and do what I've always done."

"That's not fair to her," J.R. blurted out. "She seems to know a lot."

"That just shows what you know." Jack picked up his glove and ran toward the batting cage.

Stretch kicked the grass. "What are we going to do?"

"Well, I'm going to learn more about defense," Gadget said.

"Maybe I can hit you rookies some balls." Stretch picked up a Louisville Slugger bat and adjusted his grip to a semichoked position.

The whistle blew again. The High-Fives and Alex gathered around home plate. "Defense is fifty percent of a winning team," Miss Hyland announced. "To win, you not only have to score runs but also keep your opponents from scoring. That's why you need good defense."

"You guys stay with defense. I'll stick with hitting home runs and improving my fielding average." Stretch swiveled his hips, driving his toes into the dirt.

"A good defensive player is concerned with coming up with the ball more than his average." Miss Hyland stared at Stretch. "At the beginning of each play, decide that the ball is coming to you, whether it does or not. Watch the play carefully, be aggressive and keep thinking." She walked to the bleachers for a bag of balls.

The freckles across J.R.'s nose widened as he smiled. "Sounds like she knows what she's talking about."

"She probably read it somewhere." Stretch let the bat tip drop to the ground.

"Give her a chance—it's only her first day. We don't even have a complete team yet," Gadget added.

"And what kind of a team will we recruit with a girl coach?"

The gang was silent.

"Chris, take second. Gadget, shortstop. Jack, third. Alex, center field. J.R., right field, and Stretch, first base," Miss Hyland said.

"You mean left field, don't you?"

Miss Hyland picked up a bat and ball. "No, I mean first base."

"But I always play left field."

"On this team everyone will play every position, and today you'll be playing first."

J.R. tugged at Stretch's sleeve. "Come on, it'll be fun. You're so good it won't matter, anyway."

"I guess." Stretch picked up his mitt and jogged to the unfamiliar position.

"Baseball is a game of split-second moves," Miss

Hyland said. "Think of catching and throwing the ball as one continuous motion. When catching, don't think of your glove or mitt as the 'ball catcher.' It's a tool to help *you* catch the ball, an extension of your hand." Miss Hyland tossed the ball in the air a couple of times. "At home practice catching a tennis ball barehanded so you get the feel of squeezing the ball. Right now we'll say the play is at third, so when the ball comes to you, get it to third as fast as possible."

"That's kid stuff," Stretch mumbled.

"Use both hands, and when the ball falls into the pocket of your glove, squeeze it gently. You'll close the glove automatically, and you've got the ball trapped. All right, remember the play is at third."

The team got set to catch the hit. Everyone except Stretch. He had his hands resting on his hips. Miss Hyland tossed the ball up and smacked it to center field. Alex was ready, standing on the balls of her feet, which were shoulder-width apart. Her knees were flexed, and her upper body was slightly forward. She kept her eye on the ball as it gently dropped into her mitt. Then, just as Coach Hyland had told them, she followed through by throwing it quickly to Jack at third. "Yer out!" Jack yelled as he caught the ball.

"Nice play." J.R. added.

"Way to get under the ball, Alex," Chris added.

Miss Hyland smiled. "That's the way to do it. Make sure you practice tagging up, Jack. That way it will be automatic in a game."

Jack was proud of himself. "You got it, Coach."

"Great," Stretch huffed. "Now *he's* even calling

17

her Coach. She's just a sub, and only until Coach Lehman gets back."

J.R. stepped closer to Stretch. "It was a double play."

"That's the easiest play in the book. She hardly hit it. My little sister could've caught that one."

Miss Hyland picked up another ball and knocked it directly to J.R. It sailed high, then suddenly took a nosedive and dropped. J.R. was out of position and tried to run backward to catch the ball. He held both hands up to block the fading sun. The ball landed just behind him.

J.R. slid and fell on the hard ground. "Rats."

"I got it!" Alex cried. She scooped up the error and fired it to Jack. He stretched his short legs to make the catch. It looked like he was doing the splits as he tagged the base.

"Nice recovery," Gadget called.

Coach Hyland smiled. "Alex ran to play backup. She remembered that you must always think the ball is coming to you. You never know what can happen."

Chris whistled. "That makes three outs. We're up to bat."

Stretch started to jog toward home. "Now we'll play ball."

Miss Hyland waved her arm. "Stay in your positions—we're not finished yet."

"But last year Coach Lehman always let us bat after we made three outs," Stretch called.

"I'm not Coach Lehman."

18

Stretch stopped in his tracks. "This stinks."

Coach Hyland ignored him. "Take your base."

Stretch shuffled back to his position. "I hate this."

"J.R. wasn't ready to make the play," Coach Hyland continued. "He was out of position. Check yourselves before each play. Don't be afraid of the ball. If you keep your eyes on the ball, it can't hurt you."

"But the sun was in my eyes," J.R. said.

"It'll probably be in your eyes during a game sometimes, too. Wear sunglasses if you have to, and remember that practice will teach you to adjust. If you have to put up a hand, use your arm to block the glare and keep both hands up and ready. If you have to run, J.R., turn around and run with your arms down but your eyes still on the ball. You'll move quicker and with better balance."

"Okay, I'll get it next time, Coach."

"That's the attitude."

"She's not the coach," Stretch insisted. "She's just the sub."

J.R. shrugged. "She's the best coach we've got."

"Not if I have anything to say about it," Stretch grumbled.

Chapter 3

WILD PITCH

Chris pushed open the dark green wooden door of the High-Fives' favorite hangout, Mike's Diner. "I'm dying of thirst. I'm getting three Cokes."

"That was a real workout," Jack agreed.

"I don't know which was hardest," Gadget said, "the base-running drills or the around-the-bases passing drills."

"It was the nine laps at the end that did me in." Chris smiled and staggered as if he were going to die.

J.R. sat in their booth at the back. "But it was fun. I learned a lot."

"You would've learned more from Coach Lehman," Stretch said. "He's the best. I can't believe we had to put up with her today. All those silly drills won't do any good in a real game. I'll bet Willie McGee never had to work for a girl coach. What a drag."

"I didn't think it was so bad."

Gadget rubbed his shoulder. "Me neither. I think my arm's going to be sore, but other than that I feel pretty good."

"Yeah, well, Coach Lehman would have made your arm fall off."

J.R. played with one of the spoons. "I don't want my arm to fall off. I thought it was a good practice."

"That's because you don't know better." Jack snatched the spoon from his younger brother.

"I've been playing baseball as long as you have."

"Maybe," Jack agreed. "But this is the first year you play on an intramural team at school."

"It's your first year, too."

"The difference is, I could've played last year, but I didn't want to," Jack added.

"Does that mean I get to play in the summer leagues, too?" J.R. asked.

Chris was trying to get Alex's attention. She'd come in after practice to help out her dad, who owned Mike's Diner. "If you're good enough," he said while continuing to wave a hand at Alex.

Jack leaned over his elbows on the table. "And you're not," he said to his brother.

"By the time Coach Hyland teaches me everything, I'll be three times as good as you."

Stretch jumped up from his end of the booth. "I can't believe you guys are talking about her as if she were a real coach. She's just a sub. If I have anything to do with it, she'll be a goner by the end of the week."

21

Chris tugged at Stretch's shirttail. "Take it easy, man."

Gadget motioned for Stretch to sit back down. "You two just got off on the wrong foot."

"It has nothing to do with feet. She's a rotten coach, and that's that."

"I don't know how you can say that," Gadget insisted.

"She gave us some pretty good tips about catching and stuff," Jack said.

J.R. grabbed some napkins from the holder. "Yeah, I'm not afraid of catching the ball anymore."

"I thought she made a lot of sense." Gadget folded his fingers together on the clean tabletop.

"Sense, schmense. Unless she's played competitive baseball, which I'm sure she hasn't, she can't possibly know what it's really like out on the field."

Chris leaned his head against the back of the booth. "How do you know she hasn't played baseball?"

"Get serious, she's a girl."

"So?" Alex was standing beside the table with a large pitcher of ice water.

Stretch flinched. "Geez, Alex, you scared me half to death. Quit sneaking up on us."

"I wasn't sneaking up. I help out here. Mike's my dad, remember," she added a little sarcastically.

"Well, wear a bell or something." Stretch eased back down. "You could age a guy ten years scaring him like that."

"So next time I'll play a trumpet or do a cheer."

22

"Now, that's what girls should be doing at a base-ball game. Cheering, not playing."

Alex put her hands on her hips. "What century are you from?"

Stretch stammered a little. "I meant that girls don't really play ball."

"I've been in a league for three years. My team was undefeated last year. Can you say that for your team?"

Stretch groaned. "It's not the same."

"Was it an all-girls team?" Gadget asked.

"That was the best part. We didn't have to deal with all you big-headed guys bragging all the time," Alex said.

"Come on, don't fight," J.R. pleaded. "We're all on the same team this year, and we'll still be undefeated."

"I don't know, guys. With Miss Hyland coaching, we're going to have trouble filling out the rest of the ranks," Stretch said.

Gadget was quick to answer. "Oh, no, we won't. Dan Kamer said he'd like to play short."

Chris leaned his elbows on the table. "And I heard Mike Leonard say he wants to play on a team."

"Robert Abbott said he was interested in playing. He had a dentist appointment today or else he would have been there," Gadget added.

"Remember Cathy Sullivan from our soccer team?" Alex said. "She said she'd play."

Stretch glared at her. "Don't you have something to do?"

"I was only trying to help," she said. "I was also going to ask if any of you wanted to change your usual orders, but if Stretch is going to be a jerk . . ." Alex turned and walked away.

"Don't get mad," Chris said. "I think asking Cathy is a good idea. That will give us ten players. Okay, guys?"

"Sure." Everyone nodded except Stretch.

J.R. emptied a little change out of his pockets. "I gotta change my order today, Alex. Just bring me some fries and a lot of water."

"I'll have my usual," Jack said, not willing to help out his brother.

Alex took the pencil from behind her ear. "I know, a cheeseburger, onion rings, and water. Chris will have a grilled cheese with fries and a strawberry malt. Gadget will start with a cup of minestrone, followed by the tuna platter on rye and an orange pop." Alex walked away from the table.

"Hey, what about me?"

"Normally, Stretch, I'd be happy to bring you your jumbo hot dog with the works, fries, and a Coke. But since you can't seem to be nice, you can get it yourself."

"Girls!" Stretch sighed out loud. "You can't live with them."

Chapter 4

FOUL BALL TO SECOND BASE

Stretch was all smiles when the gang met him at his locker before practice the next day. He'd decided to be a model student during history class that day. Two days of detention would be a drag. "Hey, guys, what would you get if Bo Jackson married Betty Crocker?"

"I don't know, what?" Chris was glad his friend was in a better mood that afternoon.

"A better batter. Get it? Better batter, like better cookie batter."

"We got it," groaned Jack.

"I got a million of them."

Jack slipped on his glove and gently tossed a baseball into it. "I was afraid you'd say that."

"What about this one. When does a peanut sound like a cashew?" He studied his buddies waiting for an answer. "When it sneezes."

"These are terrible," Gadget said, closing his locker door.

"Okay, how about this one. What's the first building ghosts visit when they go to New York City?"

Chris flung his jacket over his shoulder. "Is this your last one?"

"For now."

"Okay, what's the first building ghosts visit in New York City?"

Stretch grinned a mile. "The *Vampire* State Building." J.R. laughed out loud, but the others only smiled and shook their heads. "Ah-ha, I got you on that one." He slapped J.R. on the back. "I told you I got a million of 'em." The boys headed for the practice field.

"Just as long as you've got a million home runs to go along with them." Jack tossed the ball to Stretch.

"Not to worry, not to worry. Remember, you are talking to the guy who had a batting average of three-twelve last year."

"Yeah, but that was then and this is now." Red-haired Ron Porter and his buddies were blocking the exit door. Stretch was determined not to let anyone, including the Raiders, spoil his good mood. So when Randy Salazar flexed his muscles, looking a lot older than eleven, Stretch just smiled. Hank Thompson practically took up the whole doorway, but fat guys always did. Scrawny tattletale Peter Farrell wasn't far away, but as always, he was ready to take off if anything happened.

"History speaks for itself," Stretch said confidently. "Which reminds me of a joke. What did George Washington's dad say when he saw George's report card?"

Ron smirked and his freckled face looked like a dot-to-dot puzzle. "Who cares?"

"Nope. He said, 'I see you're going down in history.' " J.R. laughed again, and Jack socked him lightly in the stomach.

"That's what happens when you have a girl for a coach." Greg Forbes flipped back his longish jet-black hair. "You start telling corny jokes."

Stretch stopped laughing. "She's just a sub until Coach Lehman gets back."

Ron stepped forward, his bright blue eyes narrow slits as he glared at Stretch. "That's not what I heard. I heard she's in for the season."

"Well, you heard wrong."

"We'll see." Ron motioned for his group to follow him. "Come on, guys, let's see how many home runs we can chalk up today. *Coach* Lineweber, a real coach, says he's got a tip for us from his minor league days."

"Don't listen to him, Stretch." Chris stepped in the doorway. "You'll make twice as many home runs as he does. You always do."

"Yeah, but I wish we had Lineweber as our coach."

"Who needs him?" J.R. snatched Jack's ball from Stretch. "We've got Coach Hyland."

"Don't remind me."

27

Chris caught a toss from J.R. "Hey, she gave me a really good tip on sliding. I say she's okay."

"Look, we can't do anything about it now, right?" Jack stood with his hands on his hips. "So before we're late and have to do extra laps, I say we get to practice."

"Jack's right," said Chris. "Besides, the only way we'll beat Porter and the rest of the Raiders is to show them what the High-Fives are made of." The guys did their special group High-Five slap.

"Gather around and settle down," Coach Hyland called as the boys met her on the pitcher's mound.

Stretch was glad to see Robert, Mike, Dan, and even Alex and Cathy ready for practice. At least they had a team, Stretch thought, but would they be a winning team? That was the important question.

"I'd like you to spread out for some warm-ups before we start hitting. We have only one extra player on this team, so we can't afford any injuries."

"Warm-ups," Stretch mumbled to himself. "The next thing you know, she'll have us taking aerobics class."

Chris heard him and snickered. They both looked up and saw Coach Hyland glaring at them.

"Even though we only play seven innings, I don't want any of you fading in the sixth. Stamina will keep you going," she insisted.

"And talent," Stretch said matter-of-factly.

"Talent helps, Stretch, but lots of players have

become successful on a little talent and a lot of practice."

"Good," Gadget blurted out. "Because I have a minimal amount of talent but plenty of time to learn and practice technique. The best way I can learn to hit a ball is by thinking of science theory. You know, the shortest distance between two points is a straight line."

Miss Hyland smiled. "That's the kind of spirit we need. Now let's warm up."

The team spread out in a circle around the pitcher's mound. "Each day we'll add a few more warm-ups until they become routine and I can put some of you players in charge. Stand with your feet about shoulder-width apart. Arms overhead and grab one hand with the other. Now bend sideways at the waist and stretch. This is good for your shoulders, back, upper arms, and sides, and great for the basemen to improve their range of movement."

Stretch tried halfheartedly. "All we need now are tutus and ballet music."

Gadget nodded. "Actually, some Chopin would be nice."

"It was a joke," Stretch said, grunting through his exercises.

"It wasn't very funny," Jack groaned as he forced himself to bend a little farther.

"Now grab your left elbow with your right hand behind your head. This will stretch the back of your arm and shoulder. After about thirty seconds, switch."

Miss Hyland wandered through the group making minor adjustments. "Nice extension, Stretch."

Chris nudged his pal after she passed. "See, she likes you. She doesn't hold a grudge."

"Sit on the grass and put the soles of your feet together," Miss Hyland said. With your hands on your feet stretch forward, keeping your elbows on the outside of your knees. Hold it for thirty seconds."

"In fact, I think she likes you more than she does any of us," J.R. said.

"What makes you say that?" Stretch wanted to know.

"She mentions your name in every exercise. Stretch forward, stretch your back." J.R. laughed at his own joke.

Jack kicked his brother's foot. "What a dweeb."

"If Stretch can tell jokes, so can I," J.R. countered.

"There's only one problem," Chris said.

"What?"

"Your jokes aren't funny." The others grabbed a handful of grass and all pelted J.R. with it.

"Hey, cut it out, you guys."

Gadget laughed. "J.R., you're a nut."

"Did you say nut?" Stretch perked up. "Tell me, why did the nut cross the road?" He went into the next exercise Miss Hyland had explained. "To get to the shell station."

Jack hit his forehead with his hand. "No more, please."

"Are you having trouble with the quad stretch?"

"No, Miss Hyland." Jack lay on his back and squinted into the sun. "I'm having trouble with Stretch's jokes."

"That's enough for today. We'll add some more exercises tomorrow. Let's break into two groups and try a little pepper."

"Now we're talking ball." Stretch jumped up.

"I'd like to have pitcher tryouts at the end of today's practice, so use this time to warm up your arms."

"Maybe I can be the pitcher," J.R. said.

Jack shook his head. "Dream on. You're going to be the bench warmer."

Coach Hyland studied the group. "Stretch and Dan will be our batters."

Stretch smiled. He felt the tension in his shoulders ease some. Maybe Miss Hyland was coming around, he thought. At least she was able to recognize his batting talent. The High-Fives formed a semicircle about fifteen feet out from Stretch. The girls and the new guys went out to take Dan's hits.

"Not too hard now, fellas. Pepper is supposed to be a drill, not real play. We want to work on line drives, bunts, and grounders."

The ball felt good in Stretch's hand. He liked the way the laces formed grooves in his fingers. He picked up his favorite bat from the pile and jostled it in his hands.

"You going to use 'Red Hot' for practice?" Chris asked.

"Yep. I figured she better get used to me again."

31

Stretch tapped the first grounder. Chris stayed low, kept his eye on the ball, and scooped it up between his feet before tossing it back to Stretch.

"Nice play, Chris," Coach Hyland said, setting a bag of balls beside Stretch. "Keep them low."

Stretch picked up the next one and grounded it to J.R. The next line drive was to Jack, then Gadget caught a bouncer off a dirt clod. Stretch sighed. He was finally getting to play ball, and for the next few minutes the routine went smoothly.

"Try this one," he called, smacking a low fly ball to Jack. Stretch was getting bored with grounders and wanted to really whack a few. Before Jack had a chance to catch his ball, Stretch powered balls to both Chris and J.R. Then he put a full swing hit to Gadget in the center. All four scattered for their plays. Stretch laughed. "Caught you napping."

"What are you doing?" Gadget asked, lobbing his ball back.

"Yeah, this is supposed to be pepper. You know, easy stuff to get us warmed up."

"It's not a real game," J.R. insisted.

Jack held on to his ball. "Quit showing off and just hit us grounders."

Stretch couldn't believe his ears. "What a bunch of sissies. It takes guts to be a winning team. You guys act like you're afraid of a few hard hits."

"We're not afraid, Evans. It's just not the drill," Jack argued.

Chris walked his ball in. "Yeah, we all know

32

you're a great hitter. We just don't want to go flagging your balls."

"Okay, okay, but you're not going to get any easy grounders from the Raiders, that's for sure. Lineweber'll make 'em tough."

Coach Hyland's whistle stopped the discussion. "Let's move on to some other drills."

Stretch jogged toward left field. He was sure Miss Hyland would let him play his position.

"J.R., start at short," Miss Hyland said. "Chris, at right field. Stretch, where are you going?"

"Left field. I always play left field."

"I thought you understood that everyone will train for all the positions."

"But I don't want to play all the positions. I just want to play left field. That's where I'm good."

"Well, let's get you good at second base today."

Stretch hesitated. He could feel the anger growing inside him, and he wanted to scream at this lady, tell her she didn't know what she was talking about. Why didn't she understand? If Coach Lehman were here, or if he were on Coach Lineweber's team, he wouldn't be asked to play second base. They'd know he was an outfielder. Stretch glanced at his fellow teammates and decided they weren't going to support him. He groaned and then dawdled to second base. "What a drag."

Chapter 5

STRIKE ONE

"The purpose of playing fumble is to keep the ball going as long as possible." Coach Hyland had finished the position assignments and was giving out final practice instructions.

"I hate this," Stretch mumbled from second base. It felt awkward to be in the infield. He usually loved spring practice, but he didn't like this one at all. He had wished school were one hour a day and practice the other six. Now he kept looking at his watch, wondering when he could split. I'll bet the Raiders don't have to put up with this, he thought.

Coach Hyland continued. "This is the drill, and although you may never have to throw under these circumstances, it's worth practicing. I'll hit the ball to someone. You must catch it in your gloved hand. Then quickly flip it with that hand to the next player. Keep the ball going, because whoever has the most fumbles has to pick up all the bats and balls at the end of practice."

"Hey, Stretch." Chris nudged his buddy. "Looks like you got a fan."

"What?" Stretch was startled. He'd been trying to get the feel of the infield.

"A cheering section, or at least a fan." Chris pointed to Leena Tucker, who was lounging with another girl in the left-field bleachers.

Leena waved, and Stretch swept his fingers across the rim of his baseball cap. "She's been watching me for years."

"Kinda cute, for a girl."

"She's okay." Actually, Stretch thought it was pretty cool that Leena had come to watch him play. He was used to his folks or his sisters coming to a game, but no one had ever come to one of his practices before. He slowly raised his brown eyes in her direction. Maybe I'll flex my arms, he thought. She'll be impressed with my biceps. Stretch tried to look casual as he pushed up the sleeves of his sweatshirt. "I'll introduce you to her friend after practice if you want, Chris."

"Okay, but just to say hi."

"Whatever you say. Stick with me and they'll be following us all over school." Stretch thought this would be a good time to flex his arms. He reached his arms into the air, tensing them as hard as he could. Then he decided to widen his stance but forgot about the base. When he stepped back down on his right foot he was halfway off the base, throwing him off-balance completely. Instead of looking like Arnold Schwarzenegger, he looked like Arnold the Klutz.

For a grand finale his leg crumpled under him, and he ended up on his knees on the soft white bag.

Chris chuckled. "What are you doing?"

"Nothing." Stretch glanced over at Leena. She and her friend had their faces covered, laughing.

"Sharpen up out there." Miss Hyland picked up a bat. "Let's try for no fumbles." She tossed the ball in the air and drove it toward Cathy in right field.

"I got it!" Cathy centered herself under the ball and, with a little help from her free hand, captured the ball. She flipped it to Chris at short.

"Think fast!" Chris cried. He stretched his right leg up like a pitcher and fired the ball across the mound to J.R.

J.R. leapt for the ball that was zinging a few feet over his head. The ball bounced out of his glove, but he recovered it before it hit the dirt. "You almost got me," J.R. said over the audible sighs of his teammates. He flipped it quickly to Robert, who tossed it to Alex, who was sharing center field with Dan.

"Keep it up," Coach Hyland called with pride. Dan threw to Jack at first, and Jack side-armed a high one to Stretch at second.

Stretch knew the ball was coming to him. It looked sort of weird, though, and his instincts told him to back up. It was coming in high and fast. It'll never make the fence, he thought. "The fence." Suddenly he realized he wasn't in the outfield. That was why the ball looked so different. He'd already shifted his weight and was headed outfield, so in a flash he had to spin on the balls of his feet and stretch his arms toward the second-base bag. He groaned with effort. Like a movie in slow motion, he watched the stitches on the ball rotate closer to his outstretched glove. If he could get that last inch, he'd still have a chance at the catch. His eyes followed the ball into the glove. He pinched his fingers inside the mitt and held the leather sphere in its place as he tumbled to the ground.

"What a catch," J.R. cheered.

"Just like the pros," Jack said.

With his heart pounding like that of a scared animal caught in the headlights of a car, Stretch scrambled to his feet and, with a full-arm pitch, heaved the ball to Gadget in left field. He had instinctively put all his strength behind it. Usually he was tossing the ball from the back of left field to the catcher or one of the basemen, not to Gadget who was only twenty feet away.

"Whoa," Gadget said. The ball was so far over his head that only Michael Jordan could've caught it, and even then he would have had to be five inches taller. The ball plopped down on the left-field foul line.

"Oh, too bad," Leena said from the bleachers.

"I thought you said Stretch was good," her girl-friend said.

Leena snatched up her purse and stood. "He used to be."

"Too bad."

"Yeah, let's go." Leena led her friend away from the field.

Stretch slapped his mitt against his thigh. Everyone was staring at him. He didn't like it. Usually people stared at him because he was good. People he didn't even know would praise his talents. It was this stupid second-base stuff and a coach who made him do silly drills that was making him look bad. Stretch turned away from his team and focused his attention on the Raiders on the next playing field. They were having a scrimmage. Why can't we do that? he thought.

"I guess that fumble goes to Gadget," Miss Hyland said to Stretch. "Remember to have your target in mind before you toss."

Stretch stared at his shoes. He knew he should claim the error from Gadget, but somehow his mouth wouldn't move. It was Hyland's fault, not his. It never would've happened if he were in left field where he belonged.

Gadget cupped the ball with his glove and gently tossed it to Mike at the pitcher's mound.

Miss Hyland batted another ball to Jack at center. The rally went from Robert to Alex and Chris before Dave fumbled. No one was throwing to Stretch, and he knew it. He couldn't help but feel hurt.

Coach Hyland blew her whistle, calling the team in. "Nice drill, gang. Remember, this drill only works if you do it in one continuous motion. We'll stop now. Let's try some batting practice. Remember the rule?"

J.R. answered her. "You can't leave until you've made three base hits."

"That's right. And today anyone who's interested in being a pitcher should stay for tryouts. I'd like everyone to give it a shot, but it's not required."

Stretch picked up his bat and immediately hit three long drives. He didn't let anyone take a turn until he was done.

"Hey, don't the rest of us get a chance to play?" Jack was mad.

Stretch took that as his cue to exit. He didn't want to be the pitcher anyway. He just wanted to play left field and have a great season playing with his friends. He flung his pack over his shoulder.

"Where you going?" Gadget asked.

"I'll meet you guys at Mike's."

"Aren't you staying for the pitcher tryouts?"

Stretch glared at J.R. "You saw the way I throw. I'm not pitcher material." He shuffled his feet through the loose dirt and grass. The hurt sunk in deep and almost covered the anger he felt for Miss Hyland.

He stopped by the Raiders' field and watched them play. Ron had just hit a perfect drop ball between second and third. He'd made it to first before Peter could toss the ball to Greg at first. "Nice play," he heard Coach Lineweber say. "Keep it sharp." Now, that sounded like a coach, Stretch thought. Why couldn't Hyland be like that? He stood up and headed for the locker room. He knew he would never get used to having Miss Hyland as the coach. They didn't

39

work the same way. She would never understand
what it was like to be a real ballplayer, a star player.
One of them had to go. Stretch knew it wasn't going
to be him. Now he had to come up with a plan, a
foolproof plan. One where Miss Hyland would be the
fool.

Chapter 6

THE HALL OF FAME

Chris flung his baseball jacket on the coatrack at Mike's. "How come you left practice early, Stretch?"

"I don't want to be the pitcher. Miss Hyland said she was having pitcher tryouts."

J.R. swung into the booth. "You mean Coach Hyland, don't you?"

"No, I mean Miss Hyland. Or rather Mis-take Hyland." Stretch motioned for the gang to take their places. "I've got an idea that will solve all our problems."

"What problems?" asked Jack.

"Now look who's telling jokes. What do you mean, what problems? Miss Hyland is the nightmare of the century. That's what problem."

The gang looked at Stretch as if he were a martian.

"Where's Gadget?" Stretch asked.

The group exchanged glances. "Picking up bats

and balls with Mike Leonard. They both had two fumbles." Chris's voice was low.

"Oh." Stretch lowered his eyes because he still felt guilty about not taking Gadget's fumble. "But he is coming?"

Jack cracked his knuckles. "He'll be here."

"Good. He'll want to hear this, too."

"Well, until he gets here, I've got something to say." J.R. leaned on the table and tried to talk.

"Let's order first." Jack tapped his brother on the back. "I don't think I can take any of your great ideas on an empty stomach."

"Wait, you know the rules. No ordering before the meeting," Chris said.

"Which brings me to my idea," J.R. said, trying again.

Gadget burst in. He smiled at Stretch. "Sorry to keep you waiting."

"No problem," Stretch answered. He knew the smile meant that Gadget didn't have any hard feelings. He never did.

Chris cleared his throat. "Okay, since it sounds like we have a full agenda, let's get started. Roll call."

J.R. interrupted. "Wait, that's what I wanted to talk about."

"Not until new business," Jack snapped. "When are you going to get it straight?"

"But—" J.R. sputtered.

"No buts. Go ahead, Mr. President."

Chris spoke in a whisper. "Roll call." They all

took their right hands and made a group High-Five in the center. "Thumbs-up."

Jack tapped his thumb on the palms of the other members. "Yo."

"Index," Chris whispered.

Gadget's secret club name was Index because he was like a human index file full of information. "Present." He repeated the same motion as Jack but with his index finger.

"Center." Chris looked to Stretch.

"Cool." Stretch, as the tallest, ran his middle finger across everyone's palm.

"Ringo." Chris followed as the ringleader of the group. "And Pinkie—oops, sorry, P.K."

"Here." J.R., short for Jimmy Ray, liked being called by his initials. So even though he was the shortest and the youngest High-Five and represented the pinkie finger, he was called P.K., short for pinkie.

Each member thumped his fingers on the tabletop, high-fived the guy next to him, and wiggled his fingers. "This meeting is officially called to order."

"Finally," J.R. said. "Gadget and I have a great idea. We were looking at his computer, and he has this file on famous baseball players' nicknames. We think we should have baseball nicknames to call each other on the field."

"I've already got a nickname," Stretch announced proudly. "Home Run Stretch."

"There you go—that's perfect. And there are several other famous old-timers' names that already fit us." Gadget loved talking statistics.

"And he means old-timers. Like older than our folks."

Chris chuckled. "Did they play professional ball that long ago?"

"Some people say the game was invented by Abner Doubleday in 1839," Gadget answered.

"Is that name for real?" Chris asked.

Gadget nodded.

"Well, I don't want that to be my nickname." Jack crossed his arms over his chest.

"That's not his nickname. That's his real name. There is some controversy surrounding his influence, but most people still recognize him as the originator of baseball."

"Hey, Gadget, can I borrow that disk?" Stretch sat up straight. "If I write my paper on the history of baseball, it would help a lot."

Chris's mouth dropped open. "I thought I was writing on the history of baseball for Hyland's class."

"It's Lehman's class, and all's fair in love and war and baseball," Stretch said.

"Traitor."

Gadget tried to calm his friends down. "Maybe you can write it together. There's enough information to write ten reports."

"That's not important now!" J.R. shouted. "We were talking about team nicknames. Come on, tell them some of them, Gadget."

Gadget's grin widened. He wasn't the best athlete,

but he always knew all the rules, stats, and history of the sports they played. "These are old."

"I bet I know 'em all," Stretch bragged.

"Put your money where your mouth is, hotshot," Jack teased.

"You're on," Stretch fired back. "Whoever gets the most right doesn't pay for his meal today. The others buy."

"I don't know. . . ." Chris said hesitantly.

"What's the matter? Chicken?"

Chris reached for a pencil. "Okay, you're on."

"Does everybody have paper and something to write with?" Gadget folded his hands.

"Man, this is sounding like a test." J.R. searched his pocket for some paper.

"It is, bonehead. But this kind of test is fun," Jack said.

The boys scrambled for paper in their packs and coat pockets and even grabbed napkins to write on. "Everybody ready?" Gadget closed his eyes tight. "I'll try not to make them too hard."

"Don't hold back on my account," Stretch said confidently.

"Just write down your answers," Jack added.

"The first one is Larrupin' Lou."

"Cinch." Chris scribbled down the name. The others followed quickly except J.R.

"The next one is Casey, and the one after that is Yogi." Even J.R. wrote those down fast.

Gadget squinched his eyelids tighter. "Say Hey Kid."

45

"Hey, kid," J.R. blurted out.

"What?" Chris and Stretch said together.

Gadget repeated. "Say Hey Kid."

"I did," J.R. said innocently.

Jack sighed. "You idiot. He doesn't want you to say 'hey, kid.' That's the name of the next player. Quit being such a dork."

"I'm not a dork," J.R. mumbled. He bit the end of his eraser and wrote down a response.

"Ready for more?"

"Shoot." Chris smiled.

"Oil Can and Ho Jo."

Jack didn't even pause. "Got ya."

"Mickey Mouse and Sparky."

"Sparky sounds like a dog's name. Who'd want to be called Sparky?" J.R. laughed.

"I can't believe you don't know these," Jack groaned.

"Especially when you've already seen Gadget's disk with all the answers," Stretch added.

"I didn't memorize them. I just saw them once. Anyway, Sparky is a name for a dog, not a baseball player. Give me a break."

"Yeah, right across the nose." Jack held up his fist and circled it close.

"Quit fighting, you two. You're wrecking my concentration." Chris covered his ears to block out the noise.

Gadget kept going. "I'll give you two more and a bonus one in case there's a tie. The Yankee Clipper, Bambino, and the Sultan of Swat."

"Gross," J.R. mumbled.

Stretch eyed Gadget. "Are you sure about the last two?"

"Positive," Gadget repeated with a grin. "Time to double check."

Stretch turned his paper over. "Piece of cake."

"All right, pros, here are the answers."

"Wait a minute. Let's switch papers to check them to make sure nobody cheats," Stretch suggested.

"Some friend you are."

"There's a lot at stake here."

Chris shoved his paper to Jack. "Okay, okay, pass your answers to the right and let's get this over with."

Gadget pushed up his glasses. "Number one is Lou Gehrig."

"I got that."

"Me, too."

"The next one is Charles Stengal. Better known as Casey Stengal."

Stretch giggled. "J.R. wrote 'Casey at the Bat'."

"Well, it's not so far off," J.R. said.

Jack groaned. "It's so far off, it's on Mars."

"The next one is Yogi Berra or Lawrence Berra."

"J.R. put *Bear,* not *Berra.*"

"I still got it right."

"No, you didn't. It's not Yogi Bear. Your answer is a Boo Boo bear." Everyone laughed.

"Give him credit—it was close enough. Now, Willie Mayes is the Say Hey Kid."

Jack elbowed Chris. "How come you wrote Peter Farrell's name?"

" 'Cause I didn't know the real answer, and Peter is always saying, 'Hey. So I got it wrong.' "

"Oil Can is Oil Can Boyd and Ho Jo is Howard Johnson."

"Even J.R. got those."

"What do you mean, *even* J.R.?" J.R. asked.

"Mickey Mouse is Mickey Mantle and Sparky is George 'Sparky' Anderson."

"I'm still batting a thousand," Stretch bragged.

Jack jumped in. "Yeah, well, so am I."

"Okay. The last two are Joe DiMaggio as the Yankee Clipper and Babe Ruth as the Bambino."

"One hundred percent," Jack cheered.

Stretch snatched his sheet from Chris. "Read 'em and weep."

"Looks like we've got to use the tie-breaker." Gadget took a deep breath. "The correct bonus response is Babe Ruth."

"All right!" Stretch shouted.

"What?" Jack grabbed Stretch's paper. "That was the answer to number ten."

"It's also the bonus answer. I win!" Stretch shouted even louder.

"That's not fair," Jack grumbled. "I thought it was Roger Hornsby."

"He was the Rajah, not the Sultan. Sorry, Jack. You did really well."

"That doesn't do me any good. I still gotta buy Evans his food."

"No, you don't," Stretch said.

"How come?"

" 'Cause I'll make you another deal."

"What kind of a deal?" Jack asked warily.

"I've got a great idea on how to scare off Hyland once and for all."

Chris slumped back in the booth. "Not this again."

Gadget sighed. "Didn't you learn your lesson in detention?"

"That was nothing compared to this. Hear me out."

"Hear you out on what?" Alex stepped up to the table with her order pad.

"Nothing, Alex, just guy stuff."

"Oh, you mean you're not done with your meeting yet?"

"What meeting?" the gang said together.

"The meetings you guys are always having in here. Look, I just wanted to tell you that I put your orders in, and they'll be out in five minutes. I hope you all wanted the same stuff as always."

"Great, Alex, fine." Stretch waved her off. "Now, why don't you go away and leave us alone."

"Wait a minute," Gadget interrupted. "Alex is on the team, and if we're talking about Coach Hyland—"

"*Miss* Hyland," Stretch said emphatically.

"Whatever—she should hear what's going on."

"Brother. Okay, Alex, let me ask you something. Do you think Miss Hyland is a good coach?"

Alex shifted her weight to the other hip. "She's all right."

"But not the best, right?"

"I liked Coach Williams better."

"Ah-ha, even Alex agrees with me. We've got to can Hyland."

"I didn't say that."

"Well, I talked to Mr. Quinn, and he said he'd love to coach a team this spring. I figured if we could scare her into quitting, you know, put a little Tabasco sauce on her whistle, and a spider in her roster, stuff like that."

Gadget was stunned. "Strike one, Stretch."

J.R. laughed. "You're just joking, aren't you? You wouldn't really do that."

"Why not? It wouldn't hurt her or anything, just get her out of our way."

"I didn't think she was in our way," Alex stated.

Chris shook his head. "This has gotten way out of hand. If you'd spend more time trying to get along with her instead of trying to get rid of her, you'd play better."

Stretch stood up. "Play better? I'm the best player on the team. The only thing that's keeping me down is Hyland and maybe a few of my best friends. I thought you guys would be thrilled that Quinn wants to be our coach."

"Calm down, Stretch. No one is knocking you," Jack said.

"Doesn't sound that way to me." Stretch grabbed his jacket. I guess I'll have to do this on my own."

He stormed out of the diner before anyone could say another word.

The bell from the kitchen rang and Alex left. "I'll get your food."

The rest of the group stared at one another blankly. Finally Chris tapped his fork on the table. "Meeting's adjourned."

Chapter 7

PLAYING THE INFIELD

Chris ran up to Stretch before their special Saturday practice. "I'm really sorry about yesterday. You are the best player on our team. It's just that I hate to see you and Coach Hyland butting heads all the time."

Stretch kept walking, but he smiled. "No problem, buddy. Not after today." They joined the rest of the gang.

"Come on, Stretch, you're not still going through with that stupid plan, are you?"

Stretch stopped walking. "It's not stupid."

"I'm going to tell her," J.R. said, starting for the dugout.

"You do and you're a dead man."

"You can't talk to my brother that way," Jack added, jumping in.

Coach Hyland put the whistle to her lips and blew.

"Too late now." Stretch pulled away from Jack.

All eyes went to the coach. Her face turned red. Not just red, but fire-engine red. She dropped the whistle and held her hand up to her mouth. Stretch could hardly hide his grin. A small cough sputtered from her lips, then a little choke. Finally she sneezed. The biggest gusher the gang had ever heard. Most of the team couldn't help laughing, but Stretch and the High-Fives held it together.

Gadget offered her a tissue. "Gesundheit."

Coach Hyland took it without a word. She looked around slowly and then started to speak. "Whew, that feels much better. My sinuses were clogged this morning, but something seems to have cleared them. Must be getting close to allergy season, right, J.R.?"

Without thinking, J.R. looked at Stretch. "I guess so. I don't get allergies, though."

Jack leaned into Stretch. "Strike one, big guy. You really sent her running away with that one."

"Not to worry. That's just a warm-up for things to come. No pun intended."

Coach Hyland's voice sounded strained. "Gather around, team. There are a few roster changes I need to discuss with you before our first game with the Yanks."

Stretch elbowed Chris. "Get a load of this."

Coach flipped up the first few pages on her clipboard. "What the—?" She jumped back startled, and once again the team snickered. "Well, isn't this interesting?" Firmly she grasped the long furry leg of a gigantic spider and held it up for the team to see. "I wonder how that got in there?"

J.R. shivered. "Gross."

"Get it out of here. Those things give me the willies," Jack said.

Chris backed up. "Yuck. I hate spiders."

"There's nothing to be afraid of, is there, Gadget?" Coach Hyland asked.

"Of course not, Miss Hyland." He took the insect from her hand. "It appears to be a black widow spider."

"Drop it, man. They're poisonous," Jack said, running backward as fast as he could.

"It is also quite dead." Coach Hyland took it back and set it on the open page of her roster.

"And, if I'm not wrong, made of rubber," Gadget added.

"Rubber," Alex said.

"I knew that." Jack shrugged and tried to appear nonchalant as he walked back to the group.

Coach Hyland walked slowly around the players. "Well, I sure wish I knew who to thank."

"Thank?" Stretch asked.

"Yes, Mr. Evans. Someone has found out that one of my hobbies is entomology. The study of insects. Unfortunately, they have to be real in order to add to my collection. But this one will be fun to put with the others I do have."

"You collect spiders?" Chris asked.

"That's right. Are you the one who gave me this wonderful specimen?"

Chris glanced sideways at Stretch, then at the ground. "No way, Coach. I don't even like to touch the rubber ones."

"Then I guess it will stay a secret." She slapped the roster shut. "Start with three laps and meet me back here." She turned around quickly and headed for the dugout.

"Strike two," Jack snickered. "Who'd have guessed she liked bugs?"

"The game's not over yet." Stretch poured on the steam and sprinted ahead of the team.

"I feel kind of bad for Coach Hyland," J.R. said. "I wonder if we should've told her."

"And snitch on Stretch? No way." Jack replied. "Besides, it doesn't seem to bother her."

Chris watched his friend running. "I feel kind of bad for Stretch. He used to be a baseball superstar— now he's playing pranks and dropping catches."

"Yeah, tough luck," Gadget added.

Alex joined the group after hearing Chris. "Maybe we should do something for Stretch."

"Like what?"

"I don't know. It just seems that we should do something."

Jack ran backward. "Look, he's supposed to be great at hitting. 'Home Run Stretch,' right? When he hits some homers at the game against the Yanks, he'll forget about Hyland and be his old self again."

"Yeah, maybe you're right," Chris said quietly.

"In Stretch's own words, 'Hey, I'm always

right.' '' The gang laughed and everyone felt better. They finished the last lap and circled Coach Hyland.

"I want to give Alex as much practice pitching as possible. She's our new pitcher. Jack will sub. J.R. is going to play catcher at the game, so he'll play there today. He and Alex had nice chemistry at the tryouts."

"Woo, J.R., you and Alex have chemistry," Stretch teased.

"She means on the field."

Alex slapped Stretch's back with her cap. "Yeah, Evans, since you didn't stick around for the tryouts, we don't know *what* you have."

"Fun-ny."

Coach Hyland picked up her whistle to blow it but had second thoughts. "Settle down. The rest of the line-up looks like this. Chris at first. Mike right field. Gadget second base, and Jack at short."

Stretch could hear his heart pounding. They were halfway through the line-up, and she hadn't assigned him yet. Maybe, just maybe, today would be the day he could shine at his spot. Maybe today he'd be back in left field, where he knew he belonged.

"Robert, take center. Cathy, you'll be in left field, and Stretch, take third. Dan, we'll rotate you in, but you can start as our runner."

Stretch couldn't believe his ears. Third base. No coach would put him at third base. Coach Lineweber wouldn't. He turned around and walked slowly toward the bag. Well, it was better than first or second. At least he was on his side of the field, but when would this lady wise up?

"Hey, Stretch, going to hit a home run for me today?"

"Oh, hi, Leena. Yeah, sure. I'll hit a million."

Alex pitched low and inside for ball one.

"I've been telling all the girls what a great baseball player you are." The four girls with Leena giggled.

"Home Run Stretch, that's what they call me."

Alex sailed her second pitch in for a strike.

"How come they don't call you Third Base Stretch?" Leena asked.

Stretch sneered. "Because I don't play third base. This is just for practice."

Before he could say another word, he heard the crack of the bat and saw the ball coming right at him. It was a low grounder with a lot of hop. Instinctively Stretch snapped into a wide position and crouched down, keeping the ball aimed between his feet. It bounced low once, sideways once, and then, when it was practically on top of him, it bounce-curved toward his shoulder. He sprung back like a cat and awkwardly caught the ball. He tossed it to Chris, just missing the out.

"Way to go, Home Run." Chris tagged Dan even though he was safe.

Coach Hyland picked up a bat and got ready to swing. "The play is at second." She tapped an easy fly ball to short. Jack snatched it up quickly and hurled it back to Chris for the tag.

"Nice play, guys. Keep the pitches smooth, Alex.

We don't want you to blow out your arm in the first inning.''

Stretch watched Dan saunter home and pick up the bat. He wished he'd been assigned to be runner. He'd really show these rookies how it was done. Two more outs, and the rotation would be through.

The count went to three and two before Dan shifted his feet and sent a long drifter to Mike in right field. "Get ahead of it!" Stretch shouted.

Mike squinted in the sun, and the ball bounced six feet beyond him. He scrambled for the ball and tossed it to second, but Dan was already standing there in a puff of dust.

"Ah, man," Stretch grumbled to himself. "When you play the outfield, you've got to be a runner, a fast runner."

"I'm not a fast runner," Leena said shyly from the bleachers.

"Then I guess you wouldn't be a good outfielder. You've got to be fast."

"Oh, then you'd catch me all the time."

Stretch suddenly realized Leena wasn't talking about being a good ballplayer; she didn't even want to be one. Stretch thought it was kind of goofy, but Leena was pretty cute, and she was his first fan of the season.

"Remember the play is coming to you!" Coach shouted as she swung at an easy pitch from Alex.

The ball sailed down the center. Stretch figured it had a little top spin on it because it held the air so long. He wondered if Robert knew how to judge the ball as well as he did. In a matter of seconds the ball dropped and Robert had it tightly in his glove. "Out number two!" Stretch yelled. Then out of the corner of his eye Stretch saw Dan barreling toward him. "Robert, throw to third." Dan had tagged up after the out and was trying to play the hero.

Robert shifted his weight and strong-armed the ball toward third. Stretch had to think fast. He still wasn't used to playing the infield. My balance is all wrong, he thought. He took his eyes off the ball for an instant to make sure his right foot was firmly planted on the bag. When he looked back, Dan's eyes caught his, and his nostrils flared like those of a charging bull. It was going to be a race of seconds. The ball whizzed ahead. Stretch reached his gloved hand forward and felt the ball burn into the leather. For a second it started to drop. The bigger pocket and longer fingers of his outfielder's glove felt odd and loose. Quickly Stretch cupped his free hand over the ball and tagged Dan's elbow as he dove for the base. "Yer out," Stretch screamed.

"Double play," Alex cheered.

"Way to go, Home Run," J.R. echoed.

Dan brushed the dirt from his knees and looked at Coach Hyland for the official call. Stretch hoped she'd be honest. He'd been out by a mile. Well, not a mile, but at least a foot.

Coach Hyland's thumb jerked to the side. "You're out, Dan."

"Rats." Dan kicked the dirt and started for home.

"Stay at third," she called. "Whoever makes the

59

third out gets to come in to bat. That's you, Stretch. You're up.''

"All right." Stretch dropped his glove for Dan and jogged to home plate. He picked up Red Hot and set the bat across his shoulders, wrapping his arms around the ends. He took a few quick stretches and then planted himself about a foot from the plate.

"We're back to no outs. But I should remind you that Dan did the right thing. Tagging up and running after the second out is good strategy."

"Unless Stretch is waiting for the ball," Chris teased.

"You ain't seen nothing yet." Stretch toed in. "Hey, J.R.," Stretch whispered back at the catcher. "Why are famous baseball players always cool at games?"

The first pitch came by. "Ball one."

Stretch grinned. "Because they have fans in the stands." Alex's pitch was a little high and outside, just where Stretch liked them. He stepped forward with his left foot leading his knees and hips. His eyes watched the ball sail toward his sweet spot. His shoulders came around, and at the last second he cocked his wrists and powered the ball toward left field. He pushed off and sped toward first base like a sprinter out of the blocks. Now, this is baseball, he thought as he rounded first and pushed toward second.

Cathy backed up as far as the hedge, which marked the border of the playing field. The ball dropped in the twisted branches, and she scrambled to find it.

"Go, Stretch!" Leena and her friends cheered.

Stretch tipped his hat to them as he pounced on the third base bag and headed for the home run stretch. "Thank you, ladies." He crossed home plate before Cathy had even recovered the ball.

"Nice hit," Miss Hyland said, congratulating him. "But concentrate on the game rather than the action in the bleachers."

"Sure," Stretch mumbled. She's just jealous, he thought. He leaned against the fence while Miss Hyland prepared for the next at bat.

"I see you still got the power." Ron Porter wrapped his thick fingers through the batting cage fence. "How come she's got you playing third base, though? Doesn't she know you're an outfielder?"

"Tell me about it. How come the Raiders aren't practicing?"

"We just finished. Got a hot team, too. No left fielder with a bat like yours, but we'll still take the league."

Stretch wasn't sure why he wasn't bugged by Porter hanging out. Maybe it was because he knew baseball. "We'll see."

"Too bad you got stuck with Hyland. Lineweber's tops."

"Yeah, I know. Quinn's going to be our coach. It's only a matter of time."

"Oh, really?"

"Yep. I mean really, who could take a girl coach seriously?"

"I couldn't."

"Me, neither."

Ron grinned. "You know, you and me are a lot alike. We're winners. So, if things don't work out, maybe you can play left field for the Raiders."

"Thanks, but Quinn's going to be our coach soon." At that moment Coach Hyland connected with the next pitch, and Jack caught the bouncer in a flash at short. He tossed to Chris, who stepped on the base for the out. "I gotta go." Stretch slapped the chain-link fence and moved toward his bat. "Nice jump catch, Flash," he called to Jack. "Hey, Jumpin' Jack Flash. You just earned your nickname."

Stretch watched Ron out of the corner of his eye. Alex's arm was getting tired, and she walked Stretch in five pitches.

Stretch and Chris exchanged low-five slaps at first. "What'd Porter want?"

"Nothing. He's just watching. Actually, he was nice."

"Uh-oh. We'd better really look out, then."

"Look, Porter's not our problem. Our trouble is closer to home." Stretch nodded at Miss Hyland getting ready to bat. Normally he'd be trying to steal. Instead, he figured he'd be fast. Miss Hyland might hit into another double play. She did. A straight drive to first. Chris tagged the base and tossed it to Gadget at second. Stretch didn't have a chance. He was still two yards away when Gadget touched the bag.

"Ah!" Stretch cried in frustration. He knew he should've tried for the steal instead of talking to Chris. Now he was the third out and stuck on second

62

base while Gadget went to bat. I'll bet she did it on purpose, he thought.

Miss Hyland ran toward Stretch. "Here, try my infielder's glove. You'll get a better feel for the ball." She handed him the mitt.

"That's okay, Miss Hyland, I'm used to mine."

"No, I insist. You really should try it. I think your confidence for infield play would improve."

"No, really." Stretch knew he couldn't use the glove. He'd filled it with itching powder. If he put his fist in, the joke would be on him.

"Come on, Stretch, give it a try."

Jack tapped his shoulder. "Yeah, you're holding up the game."

Stretch gritted his teeth and slid his hand into the glove. At first he didn't feel a thing. Maybe it had evaporated or fallen out, he thought. Then, when Gadget took his first strike swing, it hit. Like a thousand mosquitoes biting at once, his hand began to itch. Just a little at first. He nonchalantly rubbed the glove against his thigh. The more his hand rubbed the leather, the itchier it got. He could feel his temperature rise, and he wanted to scream.

Gadget swung and the ball drifted to second. Stretch shook off the mitt and caught the ball barehanded on a bounce. He fired it to Chris. He had no idea what had happened. He was jumping up and down, rubbing his hand in the grass, and wiping the powder on his jeans.

Jack laughed. "What are you doing?"

"You gone crazy?" Chris asked.

63

Stretch couldn't answer. He didn't even care if he looked foolish. Anything to stop the itching. The team howled with laughter, and Leena and her friends covered their mouths to stifle their roars. Even Ron Porter was cackling from behind the fence.

"I'll be back in a minute." Stretch ran toward the school and the men's locker room. He prayed that water would cure his itch.

The coach ran up to him. "Are you all right? Did you hurt your hand with that barehanded catch?"

Stretch kept running. "No, just a little sting. I'm going to put it in some cold water to be sure. Stay here. It's nothing serious." Coach Hyland quit following him but waved in Chris to help. "Nothing serious," Stretch mumbled to himself. "Ha." This whole Hyland problem was about as serious as it could get.

Chapter 8

GRAND-SLAM BLUES

"The play's at third," Coach Hyland called as she paced along the sidelines. It was the High-Fives' first game. The top of the sixth, the Yanks were ahead six to four, and there was only one inning left.

Alex looked out of the corner of her eye before throwing the pitch. There were Yank runners on first and second. Paul, the Yank batter, was known as a heavy hitter. It didn't look good for the High-Fives. To make things worse, there were no outs. Alex couldn't walk him, because the next two batters were good, too.

Chris rocked back and forth, ready for the hit. "Remember the ball's coming to you."

Jack at shortstop slammed his fist into his mitt. "He's going to pop it up."

"Yeah, and pop-ups belong in the toaster," Stretch joked, trying to hide his nervousness. It was such a strange new feeling. When he played left field, he always knew what to do. But it was different at third base. He worried whether he'd misjudge the distance, forget to tag up, a thousand things. How he wished Miss Hyland would let him play left field. Plus, he felt as if he had to cover for Cathy as well. What was a girl doing in the outfield, anyway?

C-r-a-c-k! The bat hit the ball with a force that startled Stretch out of his thoughts. It was coming at him like a bullet from a gun. He had no time to re-adjust anything. He could let it go and hope Cathy was ready, or take the risk and go for it. His glove and free hand shot up into the air. Stretch's legs felt strong and his take-off was solid. His eyes focused on the white ball, which looked like a gray blur. Stretch was glad he had on his outfielder's glove. It would give him that extra length he was used to. Suddenly the ball hit. He could feel the leather edge of the glove tip back with the force. Slowly he gripped his palm. He had it!

"Great catch!" Cathy shouted over his shoulder.

"Yer out!" Robert cried from the bench.

Stretch's feet were heading back down when he noticed the Yank on first base tag up and head for second. He gave his legs a scissor kick to give him more time, snatched the ball out of the glove, and hurled it to Gadget at second. At least, that's where he thought it was going.

"Oh, dear," Gadget said as he jumped up.

Jack ran back a few feet at short. "What the—?" The ball was way overthrown and heading some-where between Dan at center and Mike in right field.

"Thanks," said the runner from second as he stomped on third base and headed for home.

"Cripes!" Stretch screamed as he kicked the ground. He held his glove up, hoping to get the ball so he could tag out the runner who had started on first. He caught the ball all right, but long after the runner was safe at home. The play ended in one out and two runs.

"What were you thinking about?" Jack threw his mitt to the ground.

Alex walked to third base to pick up the ball. "We could have had a double play."

Jack marched over, still angry. "A triple, if we'd played it right."

"Hey, you forget I caught the out."

"Yeah, but you let two runs by," Jack said almost in his face.

"No, *you* let two runs go home."

"How can you say that?" Jack's face was bright red now.

"You didn't catch my throw. Neither did Gadget." Stretch flung his arm toward second base. "You had two chances."

"You're crazy." Jack stepped to within inches of Stretch's nose. "The only way I could have caught that throw was if I were sitting on Gadget's shoulders."

"All right, you two," Alex interrupted. "That's enough. We can't do anything about it now, anyway."

Chris jogged over from first. "Cut it out. You're making the whole team look bad."

Jack pulled away. "No, I'm not. He is. We shouldn't call him Home Run Stretch. We should call him Stay Home Stretch. He'd be a bigger help if he did."

Coach Hyland blew her whistle and both teams' coaches converged on third base. "Break it up, boys. Let's play ball. The score is eight to four, one man out. Batter up."

Everyone shuffled back to his position. Stretch shook his head, trying to get his concentration back. This wasn't baseball, he thought, it was a nightmare. The only time people had ever swarmed him during a game was to pat him on the back or congratulate him. He hated this. He looked up at the bleachers. All the fans were shaking their heads, and even Leena looked disappointed.

"Play's at first!" J.R. shouted, trying to sound enthusiastic.

Stretch and Jack exchanged dirty looks. The batter took three swings, and the High-Fives' spirits rose with the strikeout. "Nice out, Alex!" Gadget shouted.

Stretch relaxed when the next kid stepped up to bat. He was a fifth-grader who everyone knew wasn't much of an athlete. Without thinking Stretch cupped his hands and called, "Easy out." His teammates glared at him. If looks could kill, Stretch felt as if he had been buried six feet under. He'd said it a million times before, but now it sounded wrong, all wrong.

Alex's first pitch was low and inside. "That's okay!" Stretch cried. He hoped it would help erase his other comment.

The second ball had a slight curve, and the fifth-grader swung and missed. Strike one, ball one. Alex caught him looking on the third for strike two, but the next pitch appeared to be a perfect hit. The batter connected. It was a low hopper just like the ones Hyland had made them practice. It was going directly at Gadget. Like clockwork, he set himself up and scooped under the ball for the final out.

"Just like in practice," Coach Hyland called from the side.

Stretch ran over and patted Gadget on the shoulder. "You aced the test, man. Hey, there's your new nickname, Ace."

"I like it," Gadget said proudly.

The coach quieted them down as they sat on the bench. "All right, team, we need five runs, and it's the bottom of the sixth. Wait for your pitch. Don't let the chatter get to you. Keep your concentration, and most important, have fun and work as a team."

Stretch caught Jack's eye. They glared at each other. Neither player was prepared to give in. "Mine's going out of the park," Stretch mumbled as he slid on his batting glove.

Dan was first up, and usually he was a strong, solid hitter, but that day he'd been off. This time up was no different. He popped up to center, and the High-Fives had their first out.

Cathy was up next. She was nervous, and the

Yanks could tell. "Everybody move in about sixty feet," the shortstop called. The Yanks all moved closer, hardly leaving anyone in the outfield.

"Easy out." Stretch's words echoed in his ears.

Alex knew the right thing to say. "Little hit. That's all it takes."

Cathy's first swing practically spun her around. The second was a ball. The third looked wild, but she swung at it. She hit a smooth, even swing just above their heads and dropped it between second and third. She charged through first base. The High-Fives had started their comeback. It was Cathy's first hit of the year. Stretch couldn't believe how crazy his team acted. It was just a little hit to first. Not a grand slam.

J.R. handed his brother a bat. "Bring it home."

"Just get on base," Chris added.

Jack dug his toe into the dirt and settled into the box. He practically growled at the pitcher when the umpire called the first pitch a strike. The second sailed just above his knees for the second strike, and the High-Fives became very quiet.

"Just like practice," Coach Hyland repeated.

This time the low pitch didn't throw Jack off, and he sent one to right field. Cathy moved to second, and Jack was secure at first. Once again the team was thrilled.

Now it was Chris's turn. "Keep us alive, Morton," Stretch encouraged him.

Chris was good, always relaxed and concentrated. He had a superstitious routine that he went through

HOME RUN STRETCH

before each turn at bat. He swore he'd strike out if
he didn't do it. First he rubbed a little dirt in the
palms of his hands. For friction, he said. Then he
picked up his bat and swung it around a couple of
times. Next he tapped the bottom of his shoes with
the bat. To loosen up trapped dirt, he said. Finally
he tapped the top of the plate and muttered, "See ya
soon." He took the first swing and sent the ball to
center field. Cathy made it to third in time, and the
bases were loaded.

The High-Five bench went wild. The tying run was
at bat. Gadget meekly approached the box. "I wish
it were someone else's turn."

"Confidence, man, confidence!" J.R. shouted at
him.

Stretch tried to sound supportive. "You can do it,
Ace." Unfortunately, Gadget was not the best batter.
He'd come a long way in fielding, but his swing definitely needed help. Stretch took some deep breaths
and crossed his fingers. Maybe I'm a little superstitious, too, he thought.

"Nice and easy," Alex said in a whisper. The first
swing tipped off foul to the right.

Stretch gritted his teeth. "Keep the bat level, and
crack your wrists." The second was a ball. The count
was one and one.

"That's the way to watch 'em!" J.R. boomed out.
Gadget swung at the third pitch, a fast ball, and strike
two was called.

The High-Fives' excitement had quickly changed
to fear. "Don't blow it," Stretch said under his

71

breath. He couldn't stand the thought of being on a losing team. It had never happened before. He wasn't a loser, and even though the High-Fives were his best friends, he had to be on a winning team. Before Stretch had time to think of anything else, Gadget tipped one foul, and the catcher secured it in his mitt.

It was the Yanks' turn to cheer. The bases were loaded and there were two outs. J.R. handed Stretch Red Hot, his favorite bat. "Okay, it's time to prove your name. Home Run Stretch, go to town."

Jack's phrase *Stay Home Stretch* rang in his head. If he didn't reclaim his good name now, he'd be dodging that name for the rest of the season. "One grand slam coming up." His voice cracked as he said it.

Stretch eyed the crowd with anticipation. His mom and twin sisters were sitting in the third row. Leena had stopped giggling enough to wave as he approached the batter's box. Ron Porter and the Raiders had even showed up in full force. And instead of the typical rude comment or joke, Ron flashed him the thumbs-up sign for good luck. Stretch had to squint his eyes to make sure it was really Ron.

"Batter up," the ump's low voice bellowed. The bat felt heavy in Stretch's hands. The first pitch whizzed by before he felt really set. "Strike one."

Stretch glanced at Chris on first. He was smiling encouragement. Jack seemed to be prepared to run, but his eyes were on the ground and not on the batter. A curve ball and "Strike two" from the umpire. Stretch stepped out of the batter's box. It was so quiet that he could hear the fly buzzing around his

72

batting helmet. He could feel the sweat building up on the inside of his glove. "It's now or never," he mumbled to himself. He stepped back into the box. The pitch came high and outside. Stretch could let it go, but he also knew he could connect. A split second later he swung through the air and hit the sweet spot with the power of a hurricane. It felt so easy, he thought as he dropped the bat and dashed for first.

The ball kept on going, going, going until it was out of the park. Grand-slam home run! The stands went wild—even some of the Yank players cheered without thinking. Stretch was proud to cross home plate to the applause of his teammates. The score was tied.

"Nice at bat, Stretch," Coach Hyland said. "Now, Alex, give us the winning run."

Nice at bat, Stretch thought. That's all she can say? Nice at bat? He just brought in four runs, and all the stupid coach could say was "Nice at bat." Coach Lineweber or Coach Lehman would have made him M.V.P. What did she want from him? He came to practice. He did all the requirements before he left. Okay, maybe he didn't stick around after he made his three hits, but he didn't have to. Nobody else on the team could've done what he just did. Why did she act as if it were some puny single? Stretch's stomach dropped.

Stretch uncrackled the Velcro of his glove and slid it off. He was depressed. He hadn't even noticed that Alex and J.R. had each made it on base. The only thing that caught his attention was Mike's final call from the ref, "Strike three." The score was still tied, and it was the top of the seventh. Stretch numbly sauntered to third base. He looked up only to see the first batter strike out. The second one popped out to right, and the third one got tagged at first. The High-Fives were at bat again, and Stretch hoped they wouldn't get to him in the lineup. He didn't know why, but he didn't feel like playing today. He didn't feel as if he were really a High-Five. Not today anyway.

Chapter 9

OFF-BASE

J.R. sat on the bench next to Stretch. "You've sure got what it takes. I wish I could hit a grand slam like you."

Stretch looked at him and smiled. "You will. It just takes practice."

"And talent."

"Yeah, I guess. You're a pretty good 'dogcatcher,' though."

"What do you mean, dogcatcher?"

Stretch slapped his thigh. "You know, dogcatcher, when those stray balls get anywhere near you, you snatch them up. So that makes you the dogcatcher. Pretty cool nickname for a catcher, don't you think?"

"I guess so." J.R. smiled. Cathy swung and hit. The guys watched the center fielder toss the ball to first for the out. "Too bad, Cathy. That was a great hit." Dan was out of the lineup because of a pulled muscle.

Stretch cocked his head, surprised. "She was out."

"I know," J.R. stated. "But it's the farthest she's ever hit the ball, and that should count for something. Sometimes she's the last one to leave practice. It takes her a long time to get three hits. Great job, Cathy."

"Thanks," Cathy said, coming to the bench. "That makes me feel better."

Stretch couldn't believe his ears. The girl was out, and J.R. was practically giving her a medal. Suddenly he wished for his team from when he'd been the only fifth-grader. All the sixth-graders had now gone on to junior high and new teams. Those were the good old days, he thought. Who cheered for an out?

Chris shouted from the bench. "Hit a homer, Flash!"

Jack nodded and stepped up to the plate. "One run to win." The pitcher caught him looking, and suddenly it was two outs and Chris was up to bat.

Stretch felt the old juices surge. It was miracle time. He jumped up to cheer on his buddy. "Okay, Chris, show 'em what you're made of."

Just like the time before, Chris went through his routine. He swung at the first ball and *crack,* sent it clear to the outfield bushes. A standing triple. "All right, Chris! Did you hear that crack?"

J.R. practically jumped into Stretch's arms. "I thought the bat was going to crack in half."

"That's because it was hit by 'Crackin' Chris'." He shouted the name to his friend on third base.

J.R. whispered to Stretch. "Hey, all the club members have their baseball names now. You're Home Run Stretch, Jack is Jumpin' Jack Flash, or Flash for

76

short; Gadget's Ace; Chris is Crackin' Chris; and I'm the Dogcatcher."

"Yep, we're set."

Overhearing the conversation, Jack said, "Ace is up to bat."

Coach Hyland called Gadget out of the batter's circle. "Come here a minute." They huddled and Gadget nodded his head slowly several times.

"What do you think is going on?" Jack asked.

Stretch shrugged. "Search me."

Gadget walked back to the batter's box while Coach Hyland looked to Chris. She patted her thigh twice, tapped her right shoulder, and brushed the rim of her cap.

Stretch pushed away from the fence. "I don't believe this. She's told him to bunt. Why would she tell him to bunt?"

Alex nodded her head. "I think it's the perfect plan. We all know that Gadget isn't the best hitter yet. His only chance is a bunt. The pitcher won't be ready for it. He'll probably throw the ball to first, and Chris can slip in home."

"Yeah, but even if Gadget's an ace in fielding and computers, he's not an ace at running," Stretch argued.

"They'll put him out quick as can be," Jack agreed.

"Give him a chance, you guys. Remember he's our friend," J.R. said.

The gang was quiet as they stood clutching the chain-link fence in front of the bench. "He's got to do it on the first pitch, or he'll give it away."

The pitcher sent an easy lob right over the center. Gadget held the bat firmly and slid it through his right hand. And then miraculously, just as Alex had described, Gadget was running to first and Chris was pounding toward home. The pitcher fumbled the ball twice, and when he finally tossed it to first, he overthrew. Gadget was safe by a mile, and Chris had scored the winning run.

J.R. started a chant to the stands. "Ace, Ace, Ace." Everyone repeated it over and over again, and even Coach Hyland joined in.

Realizing he was up next, Stretch picked up his bat and swung at the air. The Yanks backed up for the big hitter.

"Keep it going," Jack said.

Stretch slipped his helmet on and got into his stance. The first ball came by hard and fast, a pitcher's revenge. Stretch swung and missed. "Strike one."

The second was a knuckle ball of sorts. Another swing. "Strike two." Once again Stretch stepped out of the box to reevaluate.

"Shift your hips back and follow through." Coach Hyland's voice caught Stretch's attention.

My hips are fine, Stretch thought as he prepared to swing again. I always do it this way. The pitch came right where he liked it. His eyes focused so hard he could almost read the lettering. He swung and—"Strike three."

The game was over. The High-Fives charged out of the dugout to congratulate Gadget. Stretch stood stunned at home plate, his bat dangling in his hands.

78

Coach Hyland came out of the dugout. "That was your perfect pitch. Too bad your hips came through too early. Smooth it out and see what I mean."

Stretch looked at his mom, who smiled at him; she didn't understand. Next he glanced to where Ron and the Raiders had been. There was no sign of them. Stretch was glad they hadn't seen him strike out.

"Struck out," he muttered. "I haven't struck out in over two seasons."

"Hey, man, we won our first game." Chris pounded Stretch's shoulders. "Excellent grand slam—and wasn't Gadget awesome?"

"Awesome," Stretch repeated, still glued to his spot. Chris pulled him toward the Yank players, who were forming a line by first base. The teams carried out the traditional handshake. Stretch barely went through the motions.

"Let's celebrate!" J.R. cried.

Alex turned her cap backward. "Free root beer at Mike's."

"I can taste those winning fries already." Jack picked up his jacket and tossed his glove in the air.

Chris slapped the rim of Gadget's cap. "I'm even buying you your tuna platter. That bunt was the best."

"It was Coach Hyland's idea. She deserves the credit."

Jack gave Gadget a nudge. "Yeah, but you did it, Ace."

"Hey, and Home Run Stretch really came through

for us with that grand slam. What a way to start the season." Chris punched Stretch on the shoulder.

"Ah, that's old news for him." Jack slid his cleated shoes off. "He makes that kind of play all the time, right?"

"Next week he'll make two," J.R. added.

Robert, Dan, Mike, and Cathy waved goodbye as the High-Fives and Alex headed for Mike's. The other kids had different plans. Within minutes the High-Fives were pushing open the front door and heading for their booth.

Jack stopped dead in his tracks. "What the—?"

"Who invited them?" J.R. took off his hat and slapped his leg with it.

"We've got to do something about this and quick." Jack stood straighter and marched over to the booth.

Like fat cats, the Raiders were in the High-Fives' booth.

Jack was prepared for battle. "What do you want?"

Ron snatched a menu from the metal bracket. "I don't know. I haven't decided yet."

Greg Forbes leaned toward them. "Yeah, I hear the food here isn't too good."

"Just like the customers." Randy Salazar was trying to act really cool.

Alex took a step closer to the table. "Then why don't you leave."

"And get out of our booth," J.R. said bluntly.

"Your booth?" Ron leaned back with his hands behind his head.

Chubby Hank Thompson patted the seat. "Show me where your names are on this booth."

"Yeah, it's a free country," Ron added. "We can sit where we want."

"Well, maybe that's because you're too stupid to read." Jack snapped back.

Both groups took a tougher stance.

"Look, this is dumb," Stretch said, stepping between the High-Fives and the Raiders. "Why don't we just sit somewhere else. It's no big deal."

"No big deal?" Jack was fuming.

"You see, I always knew Stretch was the smart one. Gee, brains and a grand slam, too. Now if he could just find a team that would let him play left field, all his troubles would be solved, right?"

"He's a High-Five and that's where he'll stay," Chris said.

"Such a waste of talent. Hopeless Hyland will never understand his potential. Not like our coach. Why, Lineweber mentioned your name just the other day, Stretch, when he was giving pointers on the perfect batting stance."

Stretch perked up. "Really? What did he say?"

"Ah, he's just making it up," Jack said.

Stretch got defensive. "Why? Don't you think Coach Lineweber would brag about my batting?"

"No, he means—" J.R. stammered.

Jack tapped his brother. "I can speak for myself."

"Look, we don't want to interrupt all this good will and brotherly love. Let's split, guys." Ron and the Raiders grabbed their gear and slid past the High-

81

Fives. "Besides, I think I want to go to our place, where we know the burgers aren't made of dog food."

Alex started to lunge at Ron, but Chris held her back. "See if your dad has any disinfectant, Alex. We can't be too careful about where we sit." The High-Fives laughed and slid into their usual spots. Everyone except Stretch.

"I think I dropped something outside. Put in my order, and I'll be right back." Stretch bounded out of the diner. "Hey, Ron," Stretch called, stopping Porter at the foot of the stairs. "Did Coach Lineweber really use me as an example of a good batter?"

"You bet. We've got a couple of guys on the squad who can't quite cut it. The coach tried to explain the importance of being an all-around player, you know, MVP material, like you and me." Ron tapped Stretch on the shoulder. "He's a good coach, Lineweber."

"Wish I could say the same for Hyland," Stretch muttered.

"She's a girl—there's no chance. Look, if you ever get tired of her, I'm sure Lineweber would love a bat like yours in our lineup."

"Do you think I could play left field?" Stretch asked shyly.

"Where else?" Ron said and grinned.

From inside Mike's Diner, Gadget looked out the side window. "It appears that Stretch is talking to Porter. What do you think that means?"

Chris looked at the others. "Bad news. Real bad news."

Chapter 10

SWITCH HITTER

Chris ran down the hall to Gadget's locker, where the gang had gathered after school Tuesday. "Hey, any of you guys seen Stretch?"

"Not since history," Jack said, slamming the locker door next to Gadget's.

"Do you think he's sick or something?" Chris wanted to know.

"I don't think so, but he has been acting weird all day."

Jack slung his bat over his shoulder. "All day? Since baseball started is more like it. I think he's losing his touch."

"I wouldn't say that." Gadget took out his special blue spiral notebook from the top shelf. "According to my stats, he's batting five-fifty and his RBIs are a remarkable five."

"And that's after only one game. I don't think you can call that losing your touch."

"Something's wrong, though. That's for sure." Chris continued toward the exit. "Ever since the game yesterday, and his conversation with Porter, I don't know, something's wrong. I hate to say it, but I even miss his stupid jokes."

Jack shook his head. "Now *you're* the sick one."

"If you see Stretch, tell him I'll be out by the big oak tree next to the practice field," Chris said.

J.R. shrugged. "I'll tell him if I see him, Chris."

Alex shouted after him, "But we've only got fifteen minutes until practice! You can talk to him then!"

Meanwhile, Stretch had set his backpack on the ground and was unzipping the big pocket. He took out his outfielder's glove and his Saint Louis baseball cap, then he put in his history and math texts. He leaned against the cool brick wall of the fifth-grade wing and watched the second hand on his watch tick around. If he went to practice now, they might see him cross by the swing sets. "That won't work," he mumbled to himself. "I'll go the long way, then I'm sure to be safe." Stretch quickly zipped up his bag, flung it over his shoulder, and darted around the back toward the kindergarten playground.

Coach Hyland blew her whistle and motioned for the High-Fives to gather around the pitcher's mound for warm-ups. "We've started off the season with a win and that's good, but there were a lot of mistakes in that first game that can be eliminated with a little more thought and a lot more practice."

"Like too many pop flies."

"And overthrown tosses."

"Exactly." Coach Hyland smiled. "I've arranged a scrimmage match with the Raiders for Friday. It will give us some more actual playing time. Anybody seen Stretch? He was in school today."

"Nobody's seen him since history class," Alex said.

"Maybe he got sick and went home." J.R. said.

"He would have told me," Chris said, scowling. "We're best friends."

Gadget tried to sound optimistic. "Maybe he's only been slightly delayed."

"Let's hope so. We really need him on the team. We need everyone." Coach Hyland flipped up the first few pages on her clipboard. "Actually, it might be a good idea to recruit a few more players."

The High-Fives looked at one another. Right then they weren't worried about getting a few more players. They were thinking about just one, Stretch, and what could be keeping him from baseball practice.

Chris was put in charge of leading the warm-ups, but he didn't do well because he was so distracted. His eyes were glued to the door, which he was sure Stretch would come running through any minute.

"Let's form two lines," Coach Hyland instructed. "Face your partner and start some easy tosses. You should only be a few feet apart. After about ten catches put a little more distance between you. Keep that up until you're about sixty feet apart."

"The Little League's official distance between third and home plate," Gadget stated proudly.

"Correct. And we need the ball to travel that distance with force and accuracy." Coach Hyland tossed a ball to each pair. "I'll work with Chris until Stretch shows up."

"If he shows up," Jack muttered.

"He'll show," Chris said nervously. With each toss, though, Chris's hopes faded. Ten minutes later, when the drill ended, the High-Fives knew something was seriously wrong.

Coach Hyland blew her whistle again. "Take three laps before we start batting practice."

"Do you think he's been kidnapped?" J.R. asked as they started to jog.

"I doubt it. Why would anybody steal him?" Jack added. "It's not like his folks are rich or anything."

"Maybe they took him for his talent," J.R. suggested. "Some team could have wanted him."

Jack, Gadget, and Chris stared at one another. They all had the same idea. "It's impossible," Chris stated, not as convinced as he'd like to be.

Gadget pushed up his glasses. "Stretch is not the kind of person to defect."

"Oh, yeah? Well, I think it's the only answer." Jack slowed down as he gave his explanation. "First, he was unhappy with Hyland's coaching. Second, he wasn't thrilled about playing third base. And third—"

"You don't have to say third. He wouldn't do it.

He just couldn't. He's the one who set up the team."
Chris's voice was starting to sound frantic.

J.R. was near tears. "Do you really think Stretch
has gone over to the enemy?"

"No, you idiot." Jack punched his brother. "Not
just the enemy, the Raiders."

Chris stopped running. "Take that back."

Jack and the others stopped, too. "You know it's
true."

"We don't know anything of the kind." Gadget's
logic wasn't helping anything.

"Remember after the game when we saw him talking to Porter? What else could it be?"

"You're sick, really sick." Chris's teeth were
clenched.

Jack stepped in closer. "Not as sick as Stretch."

With one leap Chris pounced on Jack, and the two
boys tumbled to the ground. Gadget tried to grab
Chris's shoulder but fell down instead. J.R. pulled at
his brother's shirt but didn't slow him down at all.

"What is going on over here?" Coach Hyland
pulled the two apart before any real punches had
been thrown.

"Nothing," Chris said quickly.

Jack brushed the dirt from his knees. "We just
tripped when we were running, that's all."

The rest of the team had gathered at the skirmish.
"Chris, your nose is bleeding," Alex announced.

Chris wiped his nose and glared at Jack. "Yeah, I
must've hit the ground."

"Apply pressure on the vein below your nostrils,"

Gadget suggested as he handed him a handkerchief that he used to clean his glasses.

"Thanks. I'll go to the locker room and be back in a few minutes." Chris jogged toward the school.

"All right," Coach Hyland said. "It's all over now. Let's finish these laps and get on to batting practice."

Chris pinched his nose tight, and by the time he reached the locker room the bleeding had stopped. He washed his face and hands and stared blankly into the mirror. "Don't let it be true, Stretch. Don't let it be true." Chris knew he couldn't go back to practice until he had an answer. He splashed a little more water on his face and stuffed Gadget's handkerchief in his pocket.

The Raiders practiced on the other side of the school. It would take only a few minutes to find out the truth. Chris could feel his heart pounding double time as he got closer to the Raiders' field. It was hard to believe anything like this could ever happen. He thought back to all the times during soccer when Stretch had stood up to those bullies. During basketball, when he helped plan ways to outsmart those jokers. He couldn't have joined their team. The more Chris thought about it, the more confident he was that it wasn't true. Then, as he came up on the bushes next to their playing field, he heard something strange. It stopped him short.

"Hey, Porter, which fairy-tale character couldn't catch a baseball?"

"Not another one," Porter whined.

"Little Miss Muffet. You know, muffed it."

88

Chris felt as if his lunch were climbing into his throat. There was no doubt about it, that was Stretch's voice. Chris knelt on the ground and pulled back one of the branches.

"*Can* the comedy and stick to playing left field!" Greg Forbes shouted from center.

Chris was only a few feet from his friend.

"That's what I'm here for," Stretch muttered.

Chris let go of the branch and sat on the ground trying to straighten out his thoughts. Jack was right. Stretch had quit the High-Fives and was playing left field for the Raiders.

Chapter 11

TO LIVE AND DIE IN LEFT FIELD

After practice Stretch went straight home. He didn't want to risk seeing the gang in the locker room or at Mike's. He knew he'd have to face them soon—just not then. But Chris was waiting for him on the front steps of his house.

"So, when were you going to tell us?" Chris's voice sounded very bitter.

Stretch put one leg up on the first step leading to the two-story colonial house. "Tomorrow, I guess."

"Why'd you do it?"

Stretch felt a hole the size of the Grand Canyon open in his stomach. "I think it's best for everybody. Coach Hyland and I just play different ball, that's all. We're never going to see eye to eye, and besides, Coach Lineweber wants me to play left field."

"She said we needed you on the team. We do, you know."

"Nah. You forget what Jack called me. Stay Home Stretch. I think he's probably right."

Chris sat down on the top step. "That's just Jack being Jack. What about the club?"

"Hey, that hasn't changed." Stretch sat next to his friend. "I'll still be at all the meetings. I'm not going to be hanging out with those guys, just playing baseball with them."

Chris picked at a fraying thread on the cuff of his jeans. "I guess that'll work." There was a long silence. "You want me to tell the rest of the gang?"

"No, I'll do it. I'll tell them when we meet at Gadget's locker before class tomorrow morning. I'm really sorry, Chris, but it's just something I've got to do. Baseball's my favorite sport, and I've got to be on a winning team."

"The High-Fives are a winning team."

Stretch lowered his head. "I know, but I don't get to play left field, and I just think it's better this way."

"Right." Chris didn't look at Stretch as he stood up and walked down the steps. He picked up his bike and pedaled home.

"Hey, Evans!" Ron Porter shouted to Stretch the following morning before school.

Stretch got off his bike and walked over to the Bressler Elementary entrance, where the Raiders were standing in formation. "What's up?"

"Since we're playing your old team in a scrimmage on Friday, you'll have to learn our signals by then."

Greg Forbes handed him a stack of papers. "We

thought you could memorize them today at school, so we can test you at practice tonight.''

Hank Thompson's squinty eyes and piglike face pushed up close to Stretch's face. "Yeah, because you can't play if you don't know the signals."

"Put your bike down, and we'll show you before the first bell."

Stretch looked at his watch. He was already late meeting the High-Fives. He couldn't learn the signals and still explain to his pals why he was leaving the High-Fives baseball team. There wasn't enough time. "Why don't you give them to me now, and I'll go over them with you at lunch."

"Nothing doing," Ron smirked. "We can't risk having you show your buddies our secrets."

"If that's the case, what's keeping me from telling them later?"

Randy shoved his hands into his pockets. "It's not that we don't trust you. It's just that those wimps might try to pull something funny."

"Yeah, like steal the signals, make copies, and then stick them back in your backpack before you knew they were missing."

"They wouldn't do that."

"Yeah, because we're not going to give them the chance," Randy said.

"Look, you either do it this way or sit out the game. Take it or leave it." Ron was serious.

Stretch hated this. Why did they have to be playing the High-Fives? He glanced at his watch and knew it was hopeless. He'd never have the time to square

92

things now. He might as well stay here and tell the gang at lunch.

He never got the chance. At lunch the Raiders had him practice. Before classes the gang wasn't all together. Stretch wouldn't see J.R. until the day was over. "Lunch was my last chance to see them all today," Stretch mumbled to himself outside his history class. When Jack arrived, he marched right past Stretch, ignoring him.

Chris stopped in front of him. "Where were you?" "I told the guys you wanted to talk to them, and you never showed up."

"The Raiders had to talk to me about some game stuff."

"For all of lunch?"

Stretch sighed. "The Raiders practice short drills during lunch."

Chris flung his arms up in the air. "Raiders, Raiders. These guys have you hopping like a rabbit."

"It's not personal. It's just game junk."

"Well, you've got one more chance after school today before practice to explain everything to the guys."

Stretch leaned against the wall and pounded his fist into the bricks. "I can't. The Raiders are having a professional photographer come to take a picture of the team."

"Great, fine, okay, just forget it. It's pretty obvious what's happening. Look, if you don't want to hang out with us anymore, that's your choice." Chris stormed into the classroom.

"That's not it." Stretch ran after him. The bell rang and he took his seat. Why was this so hard? All he wanted to do was play baseball like he used to. Was that too much to ask?

It ended up being the longest week in Stretch's life. The only time he felt good was during practice. Not because he was a Raider, but because he felt he was doing what he did best. He was in left field again, and his fielding had improved a thousand percent, and he hadn't struck out once. The Raiders played serious ball. Not that the High-Fives didn't; it was just different. The Raiders were there to win, and Stretch liked that. He liked Coach Lineweber, too. Before he knew it, it was Friday. No one had talked to him all week except Gadget, who had discussed a science project they were doing together, and J.R., who asked him every day when he was coming back.

Ron Porter tossed Stretch a Raider's red T-shirt in the locker room. "So, did you see who they replaced you with?"

"That depends on who you think the replacement is," Greg Forbes teased.

Wiry Peter Farrell paraded around the lockers like a model. "Miss Carrie Dilley or the multi-clumsy John Heart."

Stretch's face dropped. "You mean that tall skinny guy who wears white shirts and carries pens in his pockets?"

Randy Salazar punched Stretch's shoulder lightly. "The one and only."

"Ah, geez," Stretch sat down while the Raiders continued their jokes. "That guy can't keep his socks up, so how's he going to play ball?"

"The only thing we're going to have to worry about today is if we can stop laughing long enough to hit the ball," Ron said.

Greg pulled on his shirt. "What a bunch of losers."

Stretch wanted to defend his team, but they weren't really his team anymore. It wasn't supposed to be like this, he thought. This was baseball, America's favorite pastime. The High-Fives were his friends.

"Just remember that Jack Klipp has a short temper. If we get him all riled up, he's sure to strike out." Ron added.

Randy shook his head and laughed. "And that girl pitcher. If I call her a sissy, she'll never be able to concentrate."

Stretch started to open his mouth, but his jaw froze shut. He grabbed his gear and headed for the field. "What's his problem?" Greg asked as Stretch slammed the door.

"Why do we have to play the High-Fives?" Stretch muttered to himself, running to the field. His old team was doing a little pepper warm-up practice, and they all noticed him instantly.

Jack threw the ball hard to Chris and yelled to Stretch, "We changed all our signals, so you won't be able to tell your buddies."

"I wouldn't have told them," Stretch said quietly.

"We're not even using the same batting order," Alex added.

Stretch smiled. "Maybe you'll get even better results."

J.R. looked away. "We're going to cream the Raiders."

"Look, guys, you don't understand. It's not personal," Stretch said.

Chris finally said something. "That's where you're wrong. It's very personal. Come on, High-Fives, we have a game to win."

"It's just a scrimmage," Stretch called after them.

Ron Porter slapped Stretch on the back and took him by surprise. "Hey, no contact with the enemy."

"Unless you're spying," Greg added. "Let's play ball."

The Raiders took to the field first, and Stretch couldn't believe he felt jittery. He wasn't sure whom he was more nervous for, himself or Chris, who was first up to bat. "Get a hit," Stretch said, quietly getting into position. "And, please, don't pop up to me." Just as he said it, the friends made eye contact. Chris looked determined and angry, and Stretch knew he was going to try to smack it right to him.

"Strike one," the umpire called as a fast ball burned over the plate. Ron was a great pitcher. The next pitch was a ball, and Chris got a piece of the third. Stretch's heart soared. It was an easy pop-up for Randy playing second. Out number one.

The ball rallied around the bases. "That's the way to start!" cried Greg at first.

"We'll be out of this inning in a flash," Randy added from second.

Peter laughed from third. "Piece of cake."

Hank was the last to touch the ball at catcher. The umpire took it from him and tossed it back to Ron. Gadget was up next.

"Hey, it's four-eyes."

"Maybe one of them will see the ball."

Stretch hung his head low. "Knock it out of the park," he whispered.

Gadget didn't. "Two outs," the ump called after Ron caught Gadget looking for strike three.

Alex stepped out of the on-deck circle and stepped up to the plate. "Sissy, sissy, kinda prissy, let's all call her little missy." Greg was in rare form today, and already Stretch wished he could put a gag on him.

Alex swung at the first pitch, sending it back over the batting cage. The next two pitches were balls. On the fourth fling, a low inside pitch, Alex got a piece of it and sent it toward third. Peter wasn't fast enough or tall enough to reach it, and Stretch instinctively ran into position. His gloved hand cut into the air like a hot knife through butter. He felt the leathers connect and pressed his fingers together, trapping the ball before tumbling to the ground.

"Out number three!" Ron cheered. The Raiders ran toward the bench.

Stretch slowly got up and dusted off his jeans. He'd made a great catch—so why didn't he feel great? The Raiders weren't cheering; they'd expected him to make that catch. Even worse, the High-Fives were glaring at him. Stretch tried to shake it off as he sat on the bench, waiting for his time at bat.

Ron was up first. "Better back up." He motioned for the High-Fives to get ready for a real slugger.

"Put up or shut up!" Jack hollered back.

Alex's first pitch was a strike, and Stretch secretly gloated. Ron connected on the second and sent it to Carrie in right field. It dropped about ten feet behind her, and Ron had a stand-up double before the ball reached the infield.

"All right! Way to start us off." Greg picked up his bat and tapped his shoes by the plate. Five pitches later it was strike one, ball four, and Greg was walking to first base.

Stretch rested his elbows on his knees and clasped his hands together. He rested his forehead on his thumbs. "Relax, Alex. Shake it off." He couldn't watch Randy bat. He was one of the best on the team.

"Get ready to come home," Randy bragged. The first pitch was high and inside. He swung.

"Strike one," the umpire called.

Stretch squeezed his fingers together as a silent cheer.

The next two were balls, and the third was a foul tipped toward first. J.R. hustled to catch it, but it dropped before he had a chance. "Two and two," the ump bellowed.

Alex sent the next one over the plate, and Randy caught it. As soon as the wood hit the ball, Stretch looked up to see a low grounder head toward Gadget. "Get it, Shaw," Stretch whispered. "Get it."

Gadget crouched down, and the ball hopped in front of him, bouncing toward his shoulder. It tapped him there, sending him backward, stepping on the plate. He cupped the mitt over his shoulder in time to secure the ball in the glove. Accidentally he tagged Randy, and the High-Fives had their first out.

Stretch wanted to run out and hurl Gadget on his shoulders. What a perfect play, he thought. Even if Gadget had no idea what he'd done, he'd done it, and the High-Fives were all over him. The gang even did the special High-Five sign, where they squeezed their fingers as they slapped. Stretch felt proud until Ron shouted at him.

"What are you waiting for, Evans, an invitation? You're up to bat." Ron had come home on the last play. The score was one to zip.

Stretch secured the Velcro at the wrist of his batting gloves. He picked up Red Hot and rolled her gently in his hands. He'd decided to shut out any sounds from either team and just bat. He stepped up to the plate and looked out at Alex. It was hard to think of her as the enemy.

"Okay, Evans, show us why we stole you away." Ron leaned on the chain-link fence. "Knock it out of the park."

Stretch dug his toe into the dirt. Stole me away? he thought. Nobody stole me away from anything. He didn't like the idea that anybody had that kind of power over him. He stepped out of the box and glared at Porter and then at Coach Lineweber. He hadn't really been much of a coach, so far. He was

99

always late, rarely praised the players, but jumped all over them when they made mistakes. His gruff manner matched his husky body and win-at-all-costs attitude. He was definitely different from Coach Hyland. For a moment he considered striking out just to show Ron who was boss, but he figured the coach'd replace him. Besides, he had to play his game. That was the reason for the switch in the first place. Stretch was confused. Nothing was turning out right. He stepped back into the batter's box and swung at the first pitch. It sailed over the High-Fives' heads and dropped between Jack at short and Robert in center field. Greg scored and Stretch stopped at first with Chris. They didn't say a word.

The rest of the game continued much as the first inning. No really big plays. The Raiders continued to outplay the High-Fives, and Stretch continued to get more confused. He was having a great day as far as the stats were concerned. One home run, two stolen bases, five hits, and four RBIs. It didn't feel right, though. He felt like a man without a team. Sure, he was playing better and didn't feel that tension like before, but this wasn't what he wanted, either. He tried to tell himself it was because it was his first game, or because they were playing the High-Fives. It would be different later, he thought. By the bottom of the sixth inning the score was Raiders 14, High-Fives 6.

Ron, who was the captain, snapped his fingers in front of Stretch's nose. "Hey, dreamer. You're at bat again."

"Since it's practically the last inning, I figured the coach would put in David or Scott—they haven't played all day."

Ron glanced at the duo sitting at the end of the bench. "Well, you figured wrong. Lineweber just uses them as subs. They play only if one of us real guys gets hurt. Now, get moving."

Stretch looked at the two pathetic boys who rounded out the Raiders' squad. "Sorry." At least the High-Fives let everybody play in each game. He prepared to bat, but this time the High-Fives were different.

"Strike him out!" J.R. tossed the ball to Alex.

"Burn him!" Jack echoed.

Gadget pushed up his glasses. "Use the curve ball!"

Stretch was stunned. Gadget knew he had trouble with that pitch. And why would J.R. and Jack say something so mean?

It was Chris's comment that really hurt him, though. "Easy out!"

Stretch was frazzled and took the first three pitches and struck out. It retired the side. He ran to his position and felt as if his world were coming to an end. Maybe it was.

Chapter 12

THE LAST OUT

The scrimmage ended unceremoniously. The Raiders had won, 14–6. Even though it was just a scrimmage the coaches insisted on the traditional handshake between teams. None of the High-Fives shook Stretch's hand. Instead, they either pulled away or let their fingers slide through. Stretch felt miserable and sat on the bench with his face buried in his hands while both teams headed for the showers.

"You had a good game today." Coach Hyland said proudly.

Stretch looked up at her, shocked. "It was okay."

"It was excellent. Your fielding was right on target. You really shine in left field. But I guess you already knew that."

Stretch wanted to ask her why she didn't let him play there, but that wasn't what came out. "I struck out, too, you know."

"That's because of those hips of yours. You're

forcing your knees to shift first. It's causing you to pull the bat back and swing too late. Come on, stand up, and I'll show you what I mean."

"But you're not my coach."

"That's true. I didn't know I had to be your coach to give you a few pointers. It'd be too bad if a good player like you got in a slump just because his hips were slow." She smiled and handed Stretch his bat.

Numbly he stood up and took a few practice swings.

"There it is." Miss Hyland held his shoulders, keeping him from swinging. "Now look where your hips are. It only seems to happen when you're tired or distracted."

Stretch pulled away. "I'm not tired, and no one's distracting me."

Miss Hyland nodded her head slowly. "Well, I may be wrong, but all I'm trying to say is that it doesn't happen all the time. You may want to reevaluate the circumstances. Let me pitch you a few, and then I'll leave you alone."

"That's okay." Stretch didn't want her to pitch him any, but she marched to the mound and kept coaching.

"Raise your elbows a tad. Here it comes."

The first pitch was a strong one, and it caught Stretch by surprise. The ball hit the fence of the batting cage and echoed across the playing field.

"Don't change your stance. I've got a bag of balls out here. Now get set for the next pitch."

Stretch wasn't going to let this one get by. He kept

his hands at the end of the bat. His arms were firm holding the bat above his shoulders. His knees were bent and his weight slightly shifted. It was perfect, he thought to himself. He took a practice swing and noticed that his hips were slow. He made an adjustment, and when the pitch came, he knocked it to the hedge.

"That's more like it. Now try another." She pitched three more balls, each of which Stretch sent into the outfield. "Try that at practice before your game tomorrow. I'll bet you add two more homers and no strikeouts."

"Thanks, Miss Hyland." Stretch ran to retrieve his balls.

"Glad to help out." She gathered the last of the equipment by the bench.

Stretch ran back from the outfield. "Why are you helping me, Miss Hyland? I haven't exactly been your biggest supporter."

She set down the bag and looked Stretch squarely in the eyes. "You're one of the most talented kids in the league. Other than a few of your Raider teammates, no one can even get close to your abilities. But sometimes raw talent isn't enough. That's when technique comes into play. When talent and instinct let you down, you have to have hours of practice to back you up. My father coached minor league baseball for twenty years. He said too many good players never made it big because they didn't know the total game of baseball. That's why I insisted you play the infield positions."

"I still don't get it."

She motioned for him to sit on the bench. "Let's say that you continue to be an excellent ballplayer, and one of the college teams or maybe a farm team scout sees you play."

"The Cubs. I'm going to play for the Cubs."

She sat next to him. "All right, the Cubs, but the Cubs already have several excellent men who play left field. They're going to want you to play another position."

"But I'm the best."

"Maybe. But since you're the new guy, they want to test you out at third, or center."

"I'll play it."

"You've never played those positions. How will you know how to judge the wall in center field if you've never been there? An infielder's reactions are different from those of the guy in left field."

"You can say that again."

"You wouldn't want to blow your tryout just because you'd never been willing to try."

Suddenly Stretch felt foolish. He'd never really thought of it that way. "I guess not."

Miss Hyland slapped his back and stood up. Besides, it's all part of being on a team. You can't play baseball without a team." She picked up the supplies again and headed for the locker room.

Saturday morning Stretch was eager to play ball again. He'd thought a lot about what Miss Hyland had said the day before. If the Raiders asked him to play another position, he would. He walked onto the playing field with new determination and confidence.

Ron was stretching out with a bat. "Well, gang, we didn't get much of a workout yesterday, but I guess it was better than nothing."

"If you call that brainy kid, Gadget, better than nothing." Greg Forbes picked up a ball and pitched it to Stretch.

Stretch caught it but decided not to say anything yet. He powered the ball back to Ron. The Raiders formed a big circle and pitched the ball to one another.

"Who ever heard of a girl pitcher anyway? What a joke." Hank said.

"I didn't think that was as stupid as having a girl coach."

Peter laughed. "Yeah, I'll bet when they get their T-shirts, they'll be hot pink or something weird like that."

Stretch could feel his jaw get tighter as he clenched his teeth together. Just ignore them, he thought.

"Can you imagine what kind of instructions she'd give before a game?" Ron burned one to Stretch.

"Don't get your pants dirty," Greg said.

"Watch your language," Hank added.

"And please remember to thank the officials before you leave," Randy said, laughing.

"She's not like that," Stretch said before hurling a hard throw to Peter, practically knocking him over.

Greg took the ball out of Peter's hands and glared at Stretch. "Hey, guys, remember the play when that puny fifth-grader J.R. tried to put Randy out at home?"

"He missed by a mile."

"Yeah, but then he thought he'd get Stretch coming into second."

Hank wiped his sweaty hand on his jeans. "But he overthrew it and creamed his brother at short."

"That Jack Klipp sure is a hothead. I thought he would kill his brother," Randy said.

"They should dump him," Ron said.

"Yeah, right after they cut that Morton kid," Greg said. "Who ever told him he could play first?"

Stretch hit the breaking point. "Oh, really. I seem to remember him putting you out twice at first, Greg. He's a better first baseman than you'll ever dream of being."

Peter put his hands on his hips. "What's your problem?"

"You, Farrell. Maybe having a girl coach is a little weird, but if she spent five minutes with you, you might, just *might* be able to hit a ball farther than the pitcher's mound."

"You can't talk to us like that," Hank snorted.

"If you're going to knock the Klipp brothers, I'll talk to you any way I want. They may be half your size, Hank, but each of them plays twice as good as you'll ever play. And while I'm at it, Randy, maybe Coach Hyland has some strange rules. But at least with her, guys like David and Scott wouldn't be sitting on the bench never getting a chance."

"Coach Lineweber says that as soon as they improve, they'll play." Ron shrugged.

"What kind of coach would do that? It's crazy. How are they going to improve if they don't play? Coach Hyland practices with us all the time. She gives us suggestions. Coach Lineweber didn't even show up until game time."

Ron stopped the ball and walked toward Stretch. "Take it easy. Quit acting so strange—we're just having fun."

"You call this fun? No, thanks." Stretch broke out of the circle and picked his jacket up off the bench. You're right, I have been acting strange, and the strangest thing I ever did was quit the High-Fives to join this second-rate team." He walked away.

"I always knew you couldn't take it!" Ron shouted after him. "Go to your loser team. We don't want anybody who strikes out in a clinch, anyway."

Stretch kept walking as the Raiders called after him. He felt good inside. Really good. The first time all week. He'd been so wrong about Miss Hyland and the rest of the team. He truly missed playing with his buddies and just hanging out with them. His pace quickened. He wanted to see the High-Fives, maybe play with them in their game today. If he apologized and told them he'd been temporarily insane, maybe they'd understand and take him back. He rounded the edge of their playing field and watched them play a little pepper. They looked great in their new red, white, and blue T-shirts. Just like the Cubs, he thought. They even had their baseball names sewn on the sleeves. He smiled as he slipped on his glove and ran to the bench.

"What are you doing here?" Jack snarled.

Stretch was stunned. "Well, I thought I, uh—"

"Thought you might steal some of our strategy." Jack was definitely mad. "Sounds just like something a Raider would do."

"I'm not a Raider."

"You could have fooled me," Chris added. "You sure looked like one yesterday."

J.R. looked at the ground. "You were wearing one of their T-shirts."

"Well, yeah, but that was yesterday."

"Legally you can only play for one team," Gadget said.

"And I think you made your decision pretty clear." Chris's words cut deep.

Stretch could feel the hurt spread to every inch of his body. He was really wounded. He wanted to say he was sorry. Beg to be back on the team. But he understood that he hadn't been the only one hurt. "Good luck in your game against the Tigers." The words hardly came out. The lump in his throat was climbing. He turned around and ran. He didn't know where he was going, but right then it didn't matter. Nothing mattered.

Chapter 13

THE HOME RUN

Stretch ran to the other side of the school before stopping to slump against an old oak tree to think. As bad as he felt, he knew he deserved it. He knew he was a good baseball player, but as Miss Hyland had said, it's the team that counts. He stood there for ten minutes replaying the events of the past couple of weeks. Everything from the pranks he pulled on Miss Hyland to complaining about his positions. He'd been selfish and he'd let the High-Fives down, big time.

Stretch leaned around the left side of the tree. He could see the Raiders' field. They were going to massacre the Comets. He leaned around the right side of the tree and could make out a few shapes on the High-Fives' field. It looked like the High-Fives were up to bat first. The Tigers were a tough team. It would be a real battle. His team would need everything they had to give. "My team," Stretch said.

Deep down inside they always had been, and now more than ever he had to show them. Suddenly the answer hit him.

Stretch started running back to the High-Fives field as fast as he had run away. He didn't deserve to be one of the team members, but that wouldn't stop him from giving them his support. "I'll sit in the stands and cheer them on to the biggest victory they've ever had."

"Strike one!" the umpire shouted.

Stretch climbed up to the third row of the bleachers and sat near the end. It put him close to the batter's box. Chris was on second base, and Gadget was up to bat. "Crackin' Chris must have hit a double, nice going," Stretch mumbled. Now if Gadget could keep it together, they'd have a good start.

"Strike two."

Stretch stood up and called between his cupped hands. "Remember your science theory. The quickest journey between two points is a straight line."

Gadget stepped out of the batter's box and turned around to see who was shouting. He saw Stretch and smiled.

"Think about where you want it to go, and let your bat draw the line."

Gadget tipped his batting helmet and confidently stood by the plate. The pitch came low and outside.

"Ball one."

"That's the way to watch them."

Gadget steadied his bat and stared at the pitcher. The ball came fast and about chest high. Gadget

111

watched it hit the end of the bat as he followed through with a full swing. It was a line drive inside the foul line at first.

"Run, Gadget, run," the High-Five bench cheered. Stretch stood up in the stands and joined them. "Way to go, Ace!" Although Gadget wasn't a fast runner, he made it to first base in record time. Chris advanced to third.

Alex stepped out of the on-deck circle and took a few more practice swings. "Bring 'em home!" Jack cried.

Alex's face looked more determined than ever. She swung wildly at the first pitch for strike one.

Stretch cupped his hands again. "Little hit, Alex. That's all it takes. Relax and get a little hit."

The High-Five bench looked up to the stands to spy on their one-man fan club. "It *is* Stretch," J.R. said happily.

Jack took off his hat and scratched his head. "What's he doing here? I thought the Raiders had a game."

"They do. He looks like a High-Five to me."

"Hit it just like in practice!" Stretch bellowed to Alex.

Jack sat back on the bench as the umpire called ball two. "Doesn't sound like the same Stretch who used to practice with us, that's all."

J.R. plopped down next to his brother. "Nope. It sounds like the old Stretch who played basketball and soccer with us."

Everyone stopped talking when the sound of wood

hitting leather brought their attention toward the playing field. Alex smacked a high-flyer. But instead of an easy out, the Tigers' shortstop lost the ball in the sun, and it dropped a few feet behind him. Chris made it home. Gadget courageously slid into second, losing his glasses in the effort. Alex beat the ball to first. The High-Fives were on the scoreboard, and Robert was up to bat.

The umpire called time-out while Gadget rummaged in the dust to find his glasses. He cleaned them off and placed them back on his nose. Chris crossed over to the fence between the bleachers and the field. "What's up?"

Stretch looked down at his best friend and smiled. "Just cheering on my favorite team. Get back to your game, and don't forget to tell J.R. to check with Miss Hyland about the bunt before he bats."

"I don't get it."

"You'd better get going." Stretch switched his attention back to Robert. "Come on, Bobby, you can do it." Unfortunately, he swung on the first five pitches, fouling twice and then striking out. "Rats, one away."

Chris shook his head and ran back to the bench. "I don't get it, but I think I like it."

"Okay, Flash, do your stuff," Stretch called.

Jack gave Stretch a sideways glance and swung at the air.

"Hey, batter, batter, batter, swing." The Tiger third baseman started teasing Jack.

113

The left fielder bantered back, "He's so short, the bat's bigger than he is."

Stretch could see the muscles of Jack's neck and back stiffen with each comment. The Raiders had been right. If they could mess up Jack's concentration, Jack could blow it. Stretch had to think of something fast, something to get Jack's mind off his opponents. If I could get him to laugh, that would do it. His mouth widened to a grin, and he jogged down to the edge of the bleachers directly behind the plate.

Jack had stepped out of the batter's box and was wiping his forehead with his wrist sweat band.

"Hey, Flash," Stretch said, getting his attention. "Which fairy smelled bad?"

"What?"

Stretch smiled right at him. "Which fairy smelled bad?" He waited a beat and then blurted out, "Stinkerbell."

Jack didn't laugh, but he shook his head and smiled. Stretch knew his plan was working because Jack hadn't heard the shortstop call him a dweeb. Coach Hyland watched closely. Usually no one was supposed to talk to the batter, but Stretch could tell she knew he was helping.

"How about this one? Who leaps into tall buildings with a single bound?" Stretch slapped his hands together. "Stupid Man." Jack chuckled as he moved back to home plate.

Stretch shouted after him, "What is Superman's toughest job?"

Jack tried to wave him off.

"Remembering which phone booth he left his pants in."

Jack couldn't hold it much longer. He let out one big *ha* before swinging at a perfect pitch. It was a solid double that brought both Alex and Gadget home. The score was three to zero, and it was just the top of the first inning. Stretch felt proud. For the first time this season he truly felt like he was helping his team.

The excitement came to a quick halt when Carrie flied out to second and Dan was tagged out at first. "That's okay, team!" Stretch shouted. "Now you can show them what you're really made of. Go, defense." The High-Fives rallied to their positions and talked up the team.

"Let's keep it rolling," Chris called from first.

Gadget slammed his fist into his glove. "Brains are as good as brawn. Keep thinking."

Stretch joined in. "Remember the ball is coming to you."

Coach Hyland craned her neck toward the bleachers. She smiled at Stretch again, and he tipped his cap in return.

Matt, the Tigers' center fielder, was the first to bat. He had a reputation for being a solid hitter. Alex's pitch curved in for the first strike. The High-Fives cheered together. The second pitch wasn't so lucky. Matt sent it directly toward Alex. She ducked to the right, and the pitch bounced inches in front of Gadget at second. He missed the ball, but Jack was there as backup, and he secured it in his mitt. Seconds later he delivered the ball to Chris at first. "You're out!" Stretch cried, but the umpire saw it differently, and Matt remained at first.

Coach Hyland came out of the dugout. "Keep it together."

"Next batter, double play," Stretch added.

The High-Fives calmed down. The Tigers' shortstop bounced one to Alex, she pitched it to Gadget, and then he made it to first for the double play. The crowd went wild. Stretch felt as happy as if he'd made a home run himself. He cheered until his throat was sore. Two batters and one out later he was ready to root on the batters again.

This time the High-Fives weren't so lucky. It was a quick one, two, three out inning. J.R. had been first up to bat and felt miserable. "You'll get them next time!" Stretch hollered. J.R. shrugged his shoulders but seemed to feel better.

The Tigers' coach called a time-out to change players, and Stretch saw an opportunity he had to take.

Stretch stood up and tucked the ends of his T-shirt into his jeans. He set his hat in place. "Here goes nothing," he said out loud. He bounded down the bleacher steps and caught Miss Hyland by the batting cage.

"May I speak to you for a moment?" Stretch said, clearing his throat.

Coach Hyland looked to the team and then at her clipboard. "Sure, for a minute or two."

"I just wanted to thank you for the batting tip the

other day. You were right. My hips were way out of joint. I guess so was my nose."

"I'm glad I was able to help."

Stretch shoved his hands into his pockets and scuffed his toe in a semicircle through the dirt. "I want to apologize for being such a jerk. Not just during practice or during the games, but during class and, well, everything. I was the one who pulled all those pranks at practice."

"I know. I could see what you were trying to do."

Stretch looked up at her. "You could?"

"Having a woman coach isn't easy. I appreciate the apology. I'm glad there are no hard feelings." She flipped over a page on the team roster.

"Well, I guess you've got to get back to the team. They're playing good, huh?"

Miss Hyland tapped the eraser end of her pencil on the board. "You know, your name is still on the official High-Fives team list. I haven't gotten around to taking it off yet."

"Really?" Stretch said, looking up.

"Looks like I even ordered you a High-Fives T-shirt. It says Home Run on the sleeve. So, if you'd like to slip it on, I know a team that could sure use a good player."

"You mean it?" Stretch jumped up. "I can be a High-Five again?" He paused for a moment. "But what about the rest of the team? How will they feel about it?"

"Take a look for yourself."

Stretch turned around to see best friends holding

up his High-Fives shirt and smiling at him. "Yahoo!" Stretch leapt in the air and ran toward the dugout. He slipped on the new shirt.

"Welcome back, buddy," Chris said.

"We really missed you," Gadget added.

J.R. gave him the High-Five sign. "I just knew you couldn't be a Raider."

Jack shook his head. "Besides, I missed your corny jokes."

The umpire held up his arms and shouted, "Play ball!" They all rushed back onto the field. Stretch was heading for third base when Miss Hyland stopped him. "Are you sorry you're not playing left field?"

Stretch smiled as he slammed his hand into his mitt. "It's a team sport. I play where my *coach* tells me."

About the Author

S. S. GORMAN grew up in Greeley, Colorado, with two older brothers and two younger brothers. The family was always active in sports. Their favorites included skiing, skating, softball, golf, tennis, swimming, hiking, fishing, basketball, and football. Ms. Gorman has a B.S. degree from Colorado State University and an M.A. from the University of Northern Colorado. For the past ten years she has worked as a professional performer on stage and in radio and film, as well as writing several young-adult novels. Her other titles in *The High-Fives* series are: SOCCER IS A KICK, SLAM DUNK, HOME RUN STRETCH, and QUARTERBACK SNEAK, which is coming soon from Minstrel Books. She currently lives in New York City with her husband and two-year-old son.